D0439971

BLUE BY YOU

By Rachel Gibson

RACHEL GIBSON

BLUE BY YOU

AVONIMPULSE

An Imprint of HarperCollinsPublishers

This is a work of fiction. Names, characters, places, and incidents are products of the author's imagination or are used fictitiously and are not to be construed as real. Any resemblance to actual events, locales, organizations, or persons, living or dead, is entirely coincidental.

Excerpt from *Run To You* copyright © 2013 by Rachel Gibson.

BLUE BY YOU. Copyright © 2013 by Rachel Gibson. All rights reserved under International and Pan-American Copyright Conventions. By payment of the required fees, you have been granted the non-exclusive, non-transferable right to access and read the text of this e-book on-screen. No part of this text may be reproduced, transmitted, down-loaded, decompiled, reverse engineered, or stored in or introduced into any information storage and retrieval system, in any form or by any means, whether electronic or mechanical, now known or hereinafter invented, without the express written permission of HarperCollins e-books.

EPub Edition SEPTEMBER 2013 ISBN: 9780062247490

Print Edition ISBN: 9780062247506

10 9 8 7 6 5 4 3 2

BLUE BY YOU

Chapter One

Most Sundays in St. James Parish, you couldn't swing a cat without hitting a sinner on his or her way to Mass, which was held at one church or another every half hour from seven in the morning to seven at night. While the rest of the state of Louisiana was famous for such trivialities as jazz, crawfish, and Mardi Gras, St. James Parish held the distinction of being number three on the list of U.S. counties having the most Roman Catholics.

Glory to you, Lord.

The parish was also known for Perique tobacco and three-hundred-year-old live oaks, trees draped with fingers of lacy Spanish moss.

Mostly, though, it was known for the grand plantations dotting River Road along the Mississippi. Those antebellum mansions were a part of Southern history and brought in big tourist bucks.

Thanks be to God.

From the porch of the remodeled overseer's cottage of Dahlia Hall, Blue Butler raised her Purple Jesus and drank straight from a Mason jar. The cold grape juice, ginger ale, and vodka cooled her throat and warmed her stomach. It was Sunday, and Blue treated herself to a Purple Jesus each and every Lord's Day as her reward for a week's worth of hard work.

Amen.

The setting sun cast long, lacy shadows across the sprawling gardens of Dahlia Hall, while golden light splashed across the back of the big house. The plantation had been in Blue's family for close to two hundred years. At one time, it had been one of the biggest sugar producers in the South, second only to Esterbrook Plantation, a few miles south on River Road. While Esterbrook might have produced more sugar back in the day, the big house had never been as elegant as Dahlia Hall, the grounds never as graceful. Dahlia Hall was a striking combination of the

2

raised French Creole and Greek Revival styles, with two prominent staircases curving from the ground to the upper gallery and the fanlight entrance.

Esterbrook was just your basic classic Greek Revival. Square, with two wraparound galleries supported by numerous Corinthian columns. But one thing Esterbrook had over every other Greek Revival along the Mississippi was the sheer magnitude of the big house. It was so huge, it made people wonder if the original owner, Theodore Pennington, might have been compensating for something.

Quantity didn't always mean quality, and as Blue's great-great-great-great-grandmother, Dahlia Blue Toussaint, had always been known to say about a Pennington, "You can put a gold ring in a swine's nose, but it's still a swine."

Of course, Great-great-great-great-grandmother Toussaint would have had a conniption at the very thought of one of *her* people slurping a Purple Jesus from a Mason jar. Blue was sure the first matriarch of Dahlia Hall would find her a huge disappointment. She lived in the overseer's cottage, and her hair was a constant tangle of dark curls hanging to the middle of her back. Her feet were bare and her legs exposed in a pair of jeans shorts. Not only was she drinking spirits on the Lord's Day, but she'd dribbled Purple Jesus on her thin white T-shirt. She was no Southern lady, that was for sure.

When Blue was growing up, her dearly departed grandmother had never hidden her disapproval of denim cutoffs, which she called "no 'count, backward-trash clothes," but Blue had always loved the feel of worn-in denim and never seen the need to throw out a pair of comfy jeans because they had gotten a hole in the knee. She looked a mess today, for sure, but it was Sunday. Her only day off from Dahlia Hall.

Blue took another drink and looked out at the neatly trimmed hedges, intricate beds of flowers, sputtering fountains, and the statues in the parterre. It had taken five years and more money than she liked to count to restore the gardens at Dahlia Hall, and Blue liked to think that the next few generations of Toussaint women would understand that she'd done what she'd had to do to keep the plantation in the family. She'd grown up in the big house, but it was just too much for one person to maintain. Both physically and especially financially.

Blue By You

Great-great-great-great-grandmother Dahlia had died in a buggy accident before the War Between the States and had never worried about things like money and taxes. If the original mistress could have looked into the future at her beloved home, and seen flip-flop-wearing tourists tromping along roped-off areas, three times a day, six days a week, she would have headed for her fainting couch. Strangers staring at portraits and photographs of generations of Toussaints. Tourists traipsing through her bedroom, where she'd given birth to five sons and two daughters, only three of whom had survived to adulthood. It would have tipped her into an inconsolable swoon.

Still, this was a plantation that had been run by slave labor. Blue took another drink and rocked back in her old chair. She didn't like to think of Dahlia Toussaint as a racist, more a woman of her times. There was no history that she'd had a mean bone in her body. There was no getting around the fact, as much as some families liked to hide from it now, that slavery had once been legal in the South.

Blue felt that history should be shown and talked about truthfully, which was why she'd had ten of the original sixty-three slave cabins restored, so tourists could see that part of American history. That life at Dahlia Hall had been neither Jefferson's Monticello nor Tarantino's *Django Unchained*.

There were very few plantation homes in the parish still owned by an original family member. Dahlia Hall and Esterbrook, located only a few miles from each other, were two of the few. Esterbrook was not open to the public.

The plantation down the road was currently owned by one of the last in a long line of once-proliferative Penningtons. According to Blue's accountant and high-school friend, Carolee, Kasper Pennington lived over in Jefferson Parish, but he was often seen at Esterbrook, restoring the big house. In St. James Parish, gossip was gospel, but since she'd seen more than a few construction trucks with his name splashed on the sides, she knew it was true.

Blue leaned down and set her jar on the wooden porch. She swatted away a fly from in front of her face and squinted her eyes against the setting sun. At a River Road Society meeting five years ago, she had heard all about Kasper's return to Louisiana, his time in the Marines, and his construction company. The talk was that he began by rebuilding the Katrina-ravished lower ninth ward in New Orleans and St. Bernard Parish. Now he owned and operated several construction companies and hired a lot of former Marines to work for him.

That's what she'd heard. That and other things, too. Flattering things about his career in the Marines and not so flattering things about his personal life. About his marriages–two of them—and divorces—two of them, too—and fondness for floozies. Young floozies.

Of course, Blue hadn't actually *seen* Kasper Pennington herself. Not for a long time. Not since he'd graduated from Sniper Scout school and was home on leave. That had been twenty-two years ago when his grandmother, Miss Sudie, had still lived at Esterbrook. Twenty-two years since she'd looked into his dark eyes from across steaming pots of crawdads and felt herself flush, scalded by his direct gaze.

There were some men your mama warned you about. Some *families* that *generations* of mamas warned their daughters about. "Stay away from those morally corrupt and sugar-mouthed Pennington boys," came the warning through the generations. Which, of course, only served to intrigue generations of daughters.

Daughters like Blue.

She reached for her Mason jar, and a flash of white just past the garçonnières caught her attention. Dahlia Hall was closed, the gates locked, and the security system in the big house set. Blue straightened and raised a hand above her brow. There it was again, in the shadows of the oak allee, heading toward the family cemetery. Not fast, but at a steady pace, as if slowed by age. Blue might have thought it the ghost of her dearly departed mamaw, Julia Toussaint-Butler, come back to haunt her, if it wasn't for the church hat. Like the kind her grandmother had always worn to St. Philips, but grandmother's hat had been black and covered in black netting, with a few tasteful feathers. The hat heading toward the graveyard was red. A mass of red netting and long feathers bobbing along. Grandmother would never have worn a red church hat.

Too vulgar.

Blue stood and moved to the edge of her porch. If not for the slow pace of the red hat, she might have been alarmed. She walked down the steps as the figure opened the old iron gate to the family cemetery. Blue picked up her pace and easily caught up with the woman in the hat. Osteoporosis stooped her shoulders like a turtle, and she pushed aside a feather bobbing in front of her face as she stopped in front of Blue's grandfather's, Sawyer Butler's, weathered gravestone. Pappaw Butler had died in a hunting accident when Blue had been five, and she had little memory of him other than him laid out in his black suit and the white satin lining in his casket.

"Excuse me," she said. "Dahlia Hall is closed to the public today."

The woman turned and clutched her white blouse above her heart. "Lord-a-mercy, child," she gasped. "You scared the livin' daylights out of me."

Deep wrinkles creased a pair of dark eyes made huge by a pair of thick glasses sitting on the woman's thin nose. Red lipstick leaked into the fine lines around her mouth, and age spotted her hands. The thick braid coiled at the back of her neck had more salt than pepper.

"Can I help you?"

Her dark eyes narrowed as she studied Blue's face. "Are you Julia's girl?"

"No, ma'am. Julia was my grandmother."

The woman blinked several times, as if it took her a moment or two to comprehend. "Oh." Behind the thick glasses, her gaze narrowed further. "That would be right. Are you one of Elizabeth Ann's girls or Skeeter's?"

Sawyer III, or Skeeter, was Blue's uncle. "Elizabeth Ann is my mother, but she lives in Panama City." This woman obviously knew her family. "Uncle Skeeter lives in Baton Rouge."

"That's right, you would be Elizabeth Ann's girl. Skeeter is as gay as a French horn."

Blue crossed her arms beneath her breasts. She loved Uncle Skeeter and his partner of twenty-five years, Reggie. She opened her mouth to order the rude woman off her property even though she had always been taught to give deference to her elders.

"You are the spitting image of your grandmother," she said before Blue could respond. "Julia was a beautiful woman. We had our come-out the same year."

Blue dropped her hands to her sides. Perhaps the other woman was a bit senile and could be forgiven. "You and my grandmother were friends?"

"Hell no. We hated each other worse than wolf pizen."

Blue By You

There was only one person on the planet Mamaw hated worse than wolf poison. And the whole parish knew it. "Sudie Pennington?"

She bowed her head slightly to the left.

Sudie Pennington? Here at Dahlia Hall? Blue could have been knocked over with a feather duster and was sure generations of Toussaints were spinning under her feet. Blue turned toward the big house and the road. She couldn't make out a car from this distance, and she asked, "How did you get here, ma'am?"

"Taxi."

Blue turned back. "Is the cab waiting for you?"

"'Course not. That's too expensive. Now, if you'll excuse me, I come to pay my respects."

"To whom?"

"Julia, of course."

Blue shook her head as if to clear it. "You just said you hated my grandmother." One of them was crazy as a bedbug, and she was pretty sure it wasn't her.

"Doesn't mean I can't pay my last respects," Sudie said, as if that made perfect sense.

"She's been dead for five years." Blue pointed to the granite weeping angel to her left, with her grandmother's name inscribed in the base.

11

"I was directed by the Holy Spirit at Calvary Baptist a few Sundays back." Sudie's magnified eyes narrowed behind her glasses, as if she expected an argument. "Now scoot and give me a private moment. Your grandmother and I have some things to settle up before we meet again in front of God on Judgment Day."

That's right. Not only were the Penningtons sinners, they were *Baptist* sinners. Blue wasn't comfortable leaving Miss Sudie in her family's graveyard, but who was she to argue with "the Holy Spirit?" Besides, what could one old woman with a bad case of osteoporosis do? "I'll wait for you by the gate."

"Fine. I appreciate it." Miss Sudie moved to the stone angel as Blue took a few steps toward the entrance, then stopped. She couldn't help herself, she wanted to hear what Miss Sudie had to say. "I never cared for you, Julia Toussaint. You always had your nose so high, you'd drown in a rainstorm, and I reckon you hated me with your last breath."

Blue ducked behind her great-great-uncle Perkins's massive headstone. It wasn't really eavesdropping. An old grave marker could fall over on the old girl. Miss Sudie continued, "I reckon

I gave you reason. I'm the one who started the rumor about your shoplifting cigars at the Jupiter Five & Dime when we were ten. It didn't hurt your reputation none, but I am sorry." She paused long enough to clear her throat. "I purposely took Levester Crump from you in the tenth grade. I knew you loved him, and I hinted that I'd have relations with him if he broke things off with you."

Crump? Blue could have ended up a Crump? And who the heck were the Crumps?

"I didn't have relations with Levester. I didn't even like him, but I took him from you 'cause I was mad about the pregnancy rumor you started a week before the Crawfish Festival and ruined my chances at winning Crawfish Queen. Didn't make what I did okay. I'm sorry about that, but you should probably thank me. Levester turned out to be a no 'count drunk."

Other than the fact that the Penningtons and Toussaints were raised to dislike and mistrust each other, Blue never knew why her grandmother and Miss Sudie took the feud to a whole new level. Certainly never knew that her grandmother took mudslinging to that level.

"And you got Sawyer Butler. All the girls in

the parish were crazy for Sawyer. I was crazy for Sawyer, too. Even after I married Harmon, who was a good man and treated me right, God rest his soul. Harmon traveled a lot, and while you were in Shreveport that summer before Sawyer died, I did have relations with your husband in that shiny red Coupe de Ville you used to drive to church on Sundays. I know I should be sorry, and I'm working on it. Just like I know you're working on being real sorry about getting me banned for life from the Daughters of the Brave Confederacy. My great-grandmother was a charter member and surely rolled over in her grave that day." She paused. "We did a lot of ripping at each other over the years, but when we see each other in God's holy judgment, I don't want earthly tribulations between us. So . . . I forgive you, Julia Toussaint. For everything." She took a deep breath, then said, "You can come out from where you're hiding behind that grave marker now. I'm done."

Blue stuck her head out from behind Uncle Perkins's headstone, and all she could think to say was, "I remember that Coupe de Ville." Yuck.

Sudie moved toward her. "The seats were leather. White."

"I know." She used to ride around in the backseat and was feeling a bit disturbed.

"Real cozy."

Blue looked down into the huge dark eyes behind the glasses and the red lipstick in the creases of her lips. Now she was more than a *bit* disturbed and fought the urge to scrunch up her face.

"Would you do me the courtesy of the use of your telephone?"

But Blue was born and raised in the South and gave Sudie her best PTA smile. "Of course, Miss Sudie." Together, they headed toward the overseer's cottage, and Blue slowed her pace to match the older woman's much slower steps. The deep shadows of the graveyard and trees blended with the diminishing light of the setting orange sun. There were so many things Blue was dying to say and ask, but she'd been raised better. "Would you like a glass of sweet tea while you wait?"

"Thank you. I'm parched.

Who'd have thought she'd someday offer sweet tea to Sudie Pennington. Not her. Not anyone with a drop of Toussaint blood in them. The feather in Sudie's church hat bobbed next to Blue's jaw and the side of her neck as they walked up the porch. She found her phone next to the rocking chair and beside her Purple Jesus.

"Would you like to come in while I pour your tea," she asked, and scooped up her cell.

"I'll sit here in this chair if it's the all same to you."

"Certainly. I'll turn on the zapper so you won't get eaten alive." She handed the older woman her phone, walked to the farthest end of the porch, and turned on the fluorescent bulb that lured insects to certain death by electrocution. She glanced at Sudie and her red hat before she opened the screen door and stepped inside. The cottage had been built about ten years after the big house. But unlike Dahlia Hall, the overseer's home had been modernized. The floors and windows were original, but the plumbing, kitchen, and electricity were fairly new. She pulled out her great-grandmother's Rosemare wedding crystal and dumped ice into the footed sweet tea glass. She added a sprig of mint for color, then grabbed a set of keys off a hook next to a cordless phone screwed to the wall.

The screen door slapped the frame as she moved back out onto the porch. Miss Sudie sat in the rocking chair with the cell on one knee. "Did you get ahold of someone?" Blue asked.

"Yeah, he's on his way." Sudie took her tea, studied the glass, then took a drink. "A Toussaint would choose Rosemare. Very prissy. Pennington women prefer Lismore. It's understated."

Blue raised the bunch of keys in her hand and pointed to a control panel at the edge of the driveway to her right. "My mama always said Lismore girls were fast." The kind who got banged in the back of a Cadillac. She pushed a button on the small keypad with her thumb to open the front gates. She couldn't see the double gates from where she stood, but a green button on the control panel lit, telling her the heavy iron gates were swinging open. "No disrespect, ma'am."

"Of course not, bless your heart."

Blue bit her lip to keep from smiling and pulled an old ladder-back chair beside Sudie. She sat and reached for her Purple Jesus. "Did my grandmother win your Crawfish Queen title?" She was born and raised in the South but had never entered a pageant, much to her mother's and mamaw's disappointment.

"No. Martha Jane Morvant won that year. Your

grandmother won Catfish Queen." She rambled on about the difference between the Crawfish and Catfish pageants. She took a long drink, then added, "Martha Jane married a Yankee and moved to Ohio. The last time she came home to visit her momma, she had the most god-awful accent and was wearing white shoes in January. She forgot her raisings, and her family was naturally horrified."

"Naturally." Blue took a drink of her watered-down Purple Jesus. "Bless her heart."

The corners of Sudie's mouth slid up as she took another drink and left a deep red lip print on the family Rosemare. "You married, Miss Blue?"

Sudie Pennington knew her name. She was more alarmed than surprised. Was it possible that the older woman knew about the summer of 1991? "Divorced." That hot, sticky day after she'd just turned eighteen? "I married William Chatsworth. His people are from St. Tammany Parish, and we have a fifteen-year-old son."

"Does he live here with you?"

"During the school year, but he spends the summers with his father at their lake house." Billy loved living at Dahlia Hall as much as he loved the Chatsworth family lake house, but she worried that, someday, living in a cottage at a historical tourist attraction might wear thin on Billy. If that happened, she'd have to give thought to buying a house in the suburbs.

"You must have gotten a nice settlement."

Born in the South or not, it was Blue's experience that old ladies tended to say inappropriate things on purpose. The closer they got to death, the more inappropriate. But, "Yes. I was able to do some of the major renovations on the property after my divorce."

Miss Sudie smiled as the sound of tires on gravel reached their ears. "He's here," she said, as a pair of headlights cut through the dusky night, and a white truck with tinted windows rounded the side of the big house and continued toward the overseer's cottage. A *Pennington Construction* truck.

Blue stood without thinking. "You didn't call a taxi?"

"No."

The truck rolled to a stop, and the driver's side door opened. A light illuminated the cab as one work boot, then the other, hit the gravel.

Maybe it wasn't him.

"Kasper!" Miss Sudie said, all cheery as she rose from the rocking chair and set her tea on the ground.

Maybe he wouldn't recognize her. She'd been twenty-two years younger and about ten pounds lighter. There'd been so many females in his life, surely he wouldn't remember one scrawny teenager from all those many years ago.

"Grand-mère. What are you doing here?" He shut the truck door. His voice was older, deeper. More mature. Still smooth, and Blue felt a knot in her chest. An anxious little knot, when she had nothing to be anxious about. She didn't care one bit about Kasper Pennington.

"I hate that place you stuck me."

"I didn't stick you in Sunny Crest Estates." A beige ball cap covered his hair and cast a darker shadow across his face. He stopped at the bottom of the steps and looked up at his grandmother. He was bigger, taller than she remembered, and the shadow from his hat slid to the crease of his lips. A tiny bit of anger pulled at the anxious knot in Blue's stomach. Not a lot of anger. Not enough to fly down the steps and give him a throat chop but enough that it surprised her after all these years.

20

"I thought you liked Sunny Crest Estates."

"No, boo. It's not my home."

Boo. She wondered if Sudie knew that the old Cajun endearment had been taken over by Usher and the Kardashians and just about every teen-ager in the contiguous U.S.? Maybe Alaska and Hawaii, too.

"It has bought air and cable, so you can watch all your shows." He lifted a hand and dropped it to the side of his beige cargo pants. "You have friends there."

Sudie sniffed. "It smells like old folks."

"Jesus." He pulled the hat from his head and ran his fingers through hair still as black as sin.

"I want to go home."

He folded the hat in half and stuck it in his back pocket. Then his gaze returned to his grandmother. The light from the porch touched his nose and lips and the five o'clock shadow darkening his cheeks and strong jaw. The brows above his eyes were the same black slashes that she recalled. "It's still a construction zone, Grand-mère."

Blue stood in the darker porch shadow, and, apparently, he really didn't recognize her. Praise God.

"It's my home, boo."

Kasper sighed and looked up toward the heavens as if he'd receive help from above. He swore softly and scrubbed his face with his hands.

It was best that he did not recognize her, less embarrassing that way. Best that he not recall the day they'd spent in a three-hundred-year-old oak tree. Really, why should he remember? He hadn't been the virgin.

He dropped his chin, and his gaze lowered. Within the soft orange glow of the setting sun, his dark eyes looked into Blue's. Eyes like rich chocolate that had once made her melt like a Hershey's bar. But she was older now. Wiser. Impervious to smooth talk and smoother hands than she'd been that hot summer so long ago. Even if he had recognized her, there would be no melting of any kind.

"That's where I want to die," Sudie continued.

"You're not going to die." He sighed and looked at his grandmother. "You're too stubborn to die." One corner of his mouth kicked up a little, and his dark eyes settled on her. "Hello, Blue."

Nope. No melting. Not even a little bit.

Chapter Two

1991

Barbecues were as much a part of the Louisiana fabric as Mardi Gras, voodoo, and jazz funerals. Steaming aromatic clouds from crawdad pots floated across backyard fences and mixed with smells of ribs, spicy boudin, and sweet jasmine.

In tightly packed districts around New Orleans, neighbors opened the doors to their brightly painted Creole cottages and shotgun houses and had street barbecues. Each backyard chef attempted to outcook his neighbor while fired up with secret family recipes and fueled on beer.

Warm sunshine and humidity hung over Memorial weekend of 1991, and just after noon, Blue Butler escaped the small family brunch at Dahlia Hall and hopped into her mother's Chevy Cavalier. She wore a long floral skirt and sleeveless denim shirt, but by the time she reached her friend Carolee's house in Orleans Parish, she'd tied the denim shirt in a knot just above her navel, and the long skirt lay on the seat beside her. A pair of worn, cutoff jeans shorts hugged her butt. She and Carolee had just seen *Thelma and Louise* at a theater in the Triangle, and she was feeling like a rebel. She tore the ponytail holder and ribbon from her hair and shook her head.

Carolee's street was blocked off and crowded with long tables laden with barbecue and crawdads. Pitchers of cold beer flowed from kegs, and jazz poured from houses painted the colors of sno-balls sold on Plum Street. Blue found her friend standing in front of a table weighted with food. She stood shoulder to shoulder with her neighbors, sucking heads and pinching tails. Presenting a whole different picture than the person who'd just graduated with Blue from an all-girls prep school in the Garden District. Since the first day she'd met Carolee in kindergarten, the two had become fast friends and bonded over the injustice of conservative school uniforms.

Blue joined her friend in line, reached for a spicy crustacean, and ate like a native. The two gorged until their mouths were on fire, then dodged into a neighbor's backyard, where the kegs of Budweiser were kept on ice. They drank beer out of sight of Carolee's parents and found a piece of shade across from boiling crawdad pots. They talked about graduation, and Carolee's heading to UCLA in the fall. Blue had wanted to apply to UCLA, but her mother and grandmother had pitched a fit. Toussaint women had always pledged Kappa Alpha Theta at Tulane.

She and Carolee talked about a road trip this summer, like Thelma and Louise, but without the cops and Grand-Canyon-style ending, of course. Carolee talked about hooking up with some stranger on the road, and both she and Blue didn't think either would mind losing her virginity to someone who looked like Brad Pitt.

Or Robert Downey, Jr. Except for the drug-addict part, she'd loved him in *Less Than Zero*. Dark hair and eyes and sultry smile. With her hair like Jamie Gertz's, it was just natural that she'd have a crush on Robert.

Across the yard, she watched Carolee's neighbor stirring steaming crawdad pots as she listened to her friend go on and on about all the places they would go if they actually could get away. The neighbor shifted to the left and parted the rising steam. Through the gossamer cloud, Blue's eyes met and were held by a searing dark gaze from beneath two even darker slashes of brows. He was tall, and his black hair was short in a military buzz cut. He looked slightly familiar, but she didn't know where she would have met him.

She'd gone to an all-girls school, and she doubted he'd ever sat in the pews of St. Phillips. Just a guess, but his gaze was too direct for him to be a regular churchgoer. Too male. Too worldly. Too *knowing* to belong to any boy she'd ever met before. Maybe because he was a man, not a boy, and he looked at her like a man looked at a woman, not a girl.

She turned toward Carolee, and said, "Don't look now, but there is a man standing behind the crawdad pot. Big. Dark hair. Do you know him?"

Of course, her friend immediately looked across the yard like Blue had told her not to do. "The hot guy in the white T-shirt?"

"Geez, I said don't look."

"How can I see who you're talking about if I don't look?"

She had a point, but still . . . "Yeah."

Carolee smiled and returned her attention to Blue. "That must be Wally's friend, Kasper something."

Blue's lips parted. She'd only heard the name once. Kasper Pennington. The name fit the dark, broody French-Acadian, and she was a little shocked to see him in person.

The Toussaints and Penningtons had always hated each other. Blue wasn't sure of the exact year when the feud had started, she figured some time around the turn of the century. The nineteenth century, but she did know the fiery war had had something to do with a strip of disputed land between the two properties. There had also been whispers of a Pennington, a compromising situation, and a marriage refusal. It seemed so silly now, but at the time it had been deadly business. "Stay away for those morally corrupt, sugar-mouthed, Pennington boys," her mother and grandmother had warned her. She looked back across the yard at a living, breathing symbol of her family's two-century-old feud. He

27

lifted one cocky brow, and she turned back to her friend. "How do you know him?"

Carolee shrugged. "I don't. I just know he's friends with my neighbor, Wally Doclar." She pointed her cup at the man stirring the pot next to Kasper. "Wally's in the Marines, and he and Kasper are on leave from Camp Lejeune. That's all I know, really. I only know that because I heard my dad say something to my mom about how he was going to outcook Wally and his friend Kasper this year." She grabbed Blue's free hand. "Come on."

"Where are we going?" Blue asked as beer sloshed over the top of her red Solo cup.

"You have to meet Wally. He's hysterical."

"No. No, I don't want to meet anyone." Blue shook her head as Carolee pulled her across the grass. Too late; she stood in front of Carolee's neighbor and Kasper Pennington.

"Wally this is my friend, Blue Butler."

"It's a pleasure." Wally was on the short side. Not much taller than Blue. He had red hair, and his cheeks were flushed from the boiling water. He was kind of cute, she supposed. But nothing like the big man standing next to him. "Are you from around here?"

Blue By You

Before Blue could answer, a deeper, smooth voice answered for her. "She's a Toussaint from St. James Parish."

Blue turned and met his gaze so direct, she felt pinned by it. Pinned like a bug in a science project, and she looked away from his inspection. "That's right."

"Ah," Wally said knowingly, and wrapped his arm around Carolee. "Did you go to that snotty girl's school with fancy pants, here?"

"I'm not a fancy pants," Carolee answered through a laugh and wrapped her arms around Wally's waist. "My parents aren't rich."

Soft jazz and voices from the street carried to the backyard, while Carolee and Wally argued about money and fancy-pants schools and Carolee's dog, Pepper. Blue smiled at them and brushed a long, dark curl behind her ear. Carolee had always been more comfortable around people.

"Your mama let you out to slum, princess?"

While the cottages and slim houses in Carolee's neighborhood weren't exactly the mansions of the Garden District or plantations of River Road, they were hardly the slums. Blue turned her head, and her gaze landed on a broad, muscular chest covered in a white T-shirt. Her eyes rose past a thick neck, square jaw, and full lips to the dark eyes looking down at her. She swallowed hard. Lord have mercy. From across the yard, he'd been a good-looking guy. Up close, he made her want to smooth her hair and check her makeup. She'd dated a few times in her life. When her school held dances, they'd invited boys from Holy Cross or St. Augs.

"I'm not a princess."

His attention slid down her face and throat, then continued slowly over her breasts and bare belly. She felt his gaze in her stomach and the backs of her wrists. "You look like your grand-mère."

She'd been told that before, but for some reason, hearing it from Kasper Pennington made the tingles in her wrists spread to other parts. "Did you know my grandmother?"

He shook his head and raised his gaze to her hair. "No. Never met her, but she used to yell at me when she'd catch me hauling away old boards from your property." He returned his attention to her face. "You have her hair and eyes. Is that why they named you Blue?"

She did have blue eyes, but she shook her head.

"No. I'm named after relatives." She curtsied and fired off the names written on her birth certificate, "Blue, Louretha, Dare, Toussaint, Butler," she said.

"That's a lot of name."

She rose with a smile. "God forbid we don't include a dead cousin and keep it all in the family."

He laughed and lifted a Solo cup to his mouth. "I suppose that's fitting for a Toussaint," he said, and took a drink.

She watched his throat and his Adam's apple as he swallowed. "What does that mean?"

He lowered his beer. "Y'all have been known to marry your first cousins. Inbred as all hell."

Blue gasped as all those strange tingles pinged aimlessly through her body like a pinball machine. "That's rich, coming from a Pennington. Everyone knows that the males in your family have a fondness for liquor and a taste for their brothers' wives." At least that's what she'd always heard. "Not that I would know."

"Sure."

"Believe it or not, we have better things to do at Dahlia Hall than gossip about your family."

"Like marry your cousins and make big-headed babies?"

Weren't the Pennington men supposed to be *sugar-mouthed*? "That hasn't happened in a hundred years!" Or so. It was kind of a touchy subject, and he was purposely antagonizing her. She didn't know what to do. She felt provoked even as she felt herself sucked into his dark eyes. It was bewildering as all heck. She smiled, and asked as sweet as a pecan praline, "Just how many sister-cousins are hanging on the Pennington family tree?"

"That only happened once." He chuckled, not in the least fazed. "And everyone always said Uncle Wade wasn't right after the war on account of the bullet in his skull. His first wife died in childbirth, and Uncle Charles had died at Fort Delaware the year before. So it didn't really count."

"Of course not." She waved his explanation away with her hand. The war he referred to was, of course, the War Between the States. "What about Wilkie Pennington? He was rumored to have fathered three children with his sisters-in-law and some of his servants."

"And here I thought you didn't gossip about my family."

Oh, that's right. She took a drink, then folded

her arms under her breasts. In the warnings she'd heard all of her life about the *morally corrupt* Pennington men, no one had ever mentioned that they were too big, too handsome, and too tempting. "I might have heard a thing or two over the years."

"Did you hear that Wilkie took care of *all* his children? His daughter, Ruby Gale, was the first black woman to earn a doctorate degree from Harvard."

She'd heard that. So maybe Wilkie hadn't been a complete jerk. "That doesn't make his cheating on his wife okay."

Kasper flashed a grin, then took a drink. "You obviously have never seen a portrait of his wife, Aunt Fredericka."

She swatted a bug from her face. "Does it matter?"

"Hell yes! She looked like Brezhnev, but with bushier eyebrows and less hair."

A picture of the dour communist leader with the huge black brows popped into her head. She purposely grimaced. "I did wonder where you got that unibrow."

"I don't have a unibrow."

"Bushy, like a caterpillar is crawling across

your forehead." Now it was her turn to flash a genuine smile as he scowled. "Like a buck moth caterpillar, and you know what to do about a buck moth. Kill it before it migrates to the rest of your face." Blue might not know what to do with the strange feeling bouncing around in her stomach, but she did know a thing or two about a timely exit. "See ya around, Kasper Pennington." She turned on her heels and headed toward the front of the house. She didn't look back to see if he watched her. She didn't have to. She felt his gaze between her shoulders.

As the sun set over the Crescent City, a quick rainstorm blew through and cleared away the humidity. It lasted about ten minutes and left behind clean streets and crisp air. The tables were removed, and The Hell Raisers Jazz Band set up their sound system and broke out their brass instruments. They played Coltrane and Davis as well as blowing it up with BB King and Etta James and Stevie Ray Vaughn.

Blue stood on the edge of the crowd as the last strains of "Don't Cry Baby" echoed off the houses and the streets. She rubbed her bare arm against the evening's chill and caught a glimpse of Carolee and Wally brushing against each other as they danced in the middle of the crowd. Before one song ended, another began, with the band launching into Steve Ray Vaughn's sultry and sexy "Dirty Pool."

Blue closed her eyes and felt the music slide across her skin. She hadn't seen Kasper since the rainstorm and figured that, like some of the other wimps, he'd gone home, leaving only the diehards. The badasses. The rebels.

A warm hand pressed the middle of her back, and she felt a whisper of breath in her hair next to her ear. "Come with me," he said, and for some reason she went, compelled by his voice and big hand, into the street, to be consumed by the dance crowd.

She looked up into Kasper's dark face and the flash of his white smile. "I thought you left," he said. He'd put on a gray sweatshirt with a dark emblem on the front. "I'm glad you didn't."

He took one of her hands in his while his warm palm found the small of her back. He brought her close enough that her bare belly brushed the front of his shirt. A little tug knotted her stomach and sent those confusing little tingles through her body again. She leaned into the hard warmth of his chest as shivers of sensation, from the chilly air, his hot chest, and the anticipation of more surged through her.

"Are you cold?"

Not really. Not standing so close to him, but how else to explain her shivers. "Yes."

He stopped and whipped his sweatshirt over his head. She looked up at him as he shoved it over hers, and the smell of cedar and fresh skin surrounded her face. The heat from his body was tapped inside, and she shivered once again as she threaded her arms though the sleeves. "You're a little on the skinny side. I need to take you home and have my grandmother cook for you. She'd fill you up with gumbo, fried oysters, and okra with grits on the side. Peach cobbler for dessert."

They both knew he would never take her home, and his grandmother would never cook for her. "I'm not skinny," she argued. She'd been born and raised to watch her weight and guard against thick ankles like her great-aunt Alma Dee's, bless her heart.

"All the Toussaint woman are too skinny." He rolled up the sleeves for her, and his thumbs brushed the pulse on the inside of her wrists. "Probably all those first cousins marrying."

"Are we going to talk about who's more inbred again?"

He smiled and wrapped her against him one more time. "No. Let's talk about the smell of sweet jasmine in your hair." He lowered his face to the side of her head. "You've beautiful hair."

She felt a little hitch in her chest. "I hate my hair."

"It suits you. Soft. Wild."

No one had ever said that about her hair. Or about her, for that matter. She wasn't wild. Wasn't a rebel like Thelma or Louise. But with the hitch in her chest growing and aching, pushing and pulling her, she wanted to be. For just a little while. She curled into his chest and smelled his neck. Cool, clean, and so tempting. She laid her head on his shoulder and moved with him to the sexy strains of sax, piano, and steel guitar. His hands moved across her back, up and down. Sliding up and down to the slow rhythm of jazz, and she almost moaned out loud. Maybe it was the heat of his body moving with hers, or his hands, or the sexy beat of the music, but she gave in to the temptation of his throat. She parted her lips and kissed him. Hot. Wet. Right where his shoulder met his neck.

He sucked in a breath and pushed her away. "How old are you, Blue?"

"Eighteen." He stepped back as if he meant to step away. Away from the warm and the crazy-mixed-up feelings heating up her body and making her feel so good.

He stared down into her eyes. Not quite letting her go. "You're younger than I thought."

"I'm an adult."

"Barely."

"I'm a big girl, Kasper Pennington." She didn't want him to leave. To pull his warmth away from her. She could already feel the loss of heat. "The government thinks that I am old enough to vote and die for my country." She placed her hands on the sides of his face and looked into his eyes. "I think I'm old enough to be with you."

"There's being with me." He lowered his face and brushed his mouth across hers. "Then there's being with me." The tip of his tongue touched the corner of his mouth, and he pulled her against him. If the hard bulge in his pants was an indication, Kasper was dressed left.

"You make me ache," he whispered against her cheek.

Her too. Right in the middle of her chest. An ache that started in her heart and spread to her breasts and belly and between her legs. It pulled and tugged and turned into a full-blown heart attack. A heart attack that felt good as much as it hurt. A heart attack that tightened her nipples and made her press against his chest. He hadn't even kissed her yet, and she wanted it. So bad. She slid her hand up his hard, bare arm and over the short sleeve of his T-shirt. She parted her lips and invited him inside. His tongue brushed hers, a soft touch and light sweep, and she moaned deep in her throat. She wrapped her arms around his neck as they swayed to sensual jazz and sultry blues. She sucked him deeper in her mouth, and the kiss turned as hot as the music swirling around them. Blue was not the sort of girl to make out in public at a street dance. She'd never done it before, but she'd never felt this way before. Attractive. Sexual. Wanted by an extremely attractive man. A Pennington. He was forbidden, and she was a rebel.

His lips were so warm and firm, and he tasted like passion. Dizzy, chaotic passion, and when he pressed his erection to her, she let him. She let him because it felt so good. Hot and liquid and intoxicating. He slid one hand down her side and slipped it under the edge of his sweatshirt. His thumb brushed her bare skin just above the waistband of her shorts. The touch of his fingers on the small of her back sent tingles up and down her spine.

She ran her hands over his shoulders and neck, and the kiss got hotter and greedy. A carnal assault of lips and tongue and wet passion. Of hot bodies rubbing against each other and his hand sliding up her bare back beneath her denim shirt.

Standing beneath the full moon. She wasn't Blue Louretha Dare Toussaint Butler. Raised by her mother and grandmother at Dahlia Hall and recent graduate of an all-girls school. She was an adult. A woman on her way to Tulane in the fall. A woman who wanted to feel what every woman felt. Lust for a man. The touch of a man. Not the tentative touch of boys who had little more experience than she did.

The last strains of "Dirty Pool" floated around them, and Kasper's assault on her mouth slowed, and he pulled back. His voice was a low, soft growl when he said, "Come with me, cher."

"Where?"

"Esterbrook."

She swallowed as her dizzy world tried to focus beyond anything but the liquid passion in her body. "Why?"

He leaned down and peered into her eyes through the darkness. "Because we can't go any further on a public street without getting arrested. Not even in New Orleans."

"Oh." That wouldn't be good. If she got thrown in the slammer, her grandmother would surely pitch a fit. If she got thrown in the slammer with Kasper Pennington, it would surely kill the woman.

"I know you said you're a grown woman, but do you know where grinding against a man leads?"

Her throat closed, and she nodded. Yes. She knew. She was eighteen. A virgin, but she knew.

"Then come home with me, Blue. Let me make love to you all night." He took his hand from her back. "Let me make love until you think you can't take any more. Then I'll kiss you all over and make you change your mind." He took her hand. "Come with me."

Blue took a step back, and her hand dropped

from his. Kissing Kasper Pennington and rubbing against him in the middle of a crowded street was one thing. It was thrilling. Hot. Rebellious. Leaving with him to make love at Esterbrook was another.

She took a step back. "I can't."

Kasper turned his head to the side and looked at her. "Go, then," he said. "I don't have time for little girls."

She took several more steps back and blended into the crowd. She turned and raised a hand to her swollen mouth. She didn't feel like a girl. She felt like a woman who wanted the one man on the planet she could never have.

Nothing good would come of it. She'd be the first Toussaint descendant to fall in bed with a sugar-mouthed Pennington. All those generations of Toussaints would roll in their graves. Probably come back and haunt her.

Come with me, cher, and God help her, if he'd been anyone else on the planet, she might have done it. Might have thrown caution to the wind. But in the end, she hadn't been raised a rebel.

Chapter Three

The ancient wood creaked beneath Kasper Pennington's feet as he walked down the warped steps of Esterbrook's grand staircase. The ten-thousand-square-foot house needed work. A lot of work. At one time, there had been a lot of Penningtons living in the big house. Now there was just him and his grandmother, Miss Sudie. The two-hundred-year-old plantation house had been in Kasper's family since before the Civil War. The place had been one of the South's leading sugar producers, but now the big home sat on ten acres of mostly overgrown cypress and kudzu.

Some people looked at the old place, with its massive columns and wraparound galleries, and saw nothing but a money pit. A dinosaur around their neck. Kasper wasn't one of those people.

Growing up at Esterbrook had been amazing. He'd crawled under acres of kudzu and shot a lot of squirrels. These days, he crawled around in a Gilles suit and shot enemy combatants, but he'd gotten his early training here on the plantation. He'd just graduated Scout Sniper school and was due back at Lejeune in three days. His Hog's Tooth hung around his neck on a leather cord, and he expected deployment within weeks to Bosnia or Somalia or anywhere bad guys were acting up and needed to be taken down.

The year before, he'd been deployed to Iraq. Thank God the Gulf War hadn't been a long one because he hated that dust bowl of a county and never wanted to go back. He was grateful, though. Grateful to serve his country and have the opportunity to add a few more medals and ribbons to dress blues. Kasper loved the military life. Loved being a Marine, and had worked damn hard to earn his Hog's Tooth. His life was exactly what he'd envisioned. Exactly what he'd planned for himself. There'd been a Pennington man in every war since the American Revolution, and Kasper's feet were firmly planted on a path for military success.

Kasper ate a quick bowl of cereal and headed outside. He worked on the big house whenever he was in town, but that wasn't often lately. He sent his grandmother money for basic upkeep, but it needed more than the basics. He grabbed his Camp Lejeune ball cap and opened the back door. The old hinges creaked as he moved to a woodpile on the side of the house.

Pulling his cap farther down his brow, he picked up an axe leaning against a stump. He needed to chop enough wood to make sure his grandmother had plenty for when he wasn't around this winter. He'd tried to talk her into moving into a smaller house, a house much more manageable for a woman in her sixties. Of course she didn't want to hear a word of it.

The first chop of the axe split the log in half, and the pieces flew to the sides. It was a little after ten in the morning, and a cool breeze fluttered the leaves and Spanish moss on the live oak around the place. It was bound to get a hell of lot hotter. Like yesterday.

He put another log on the stump. When he'd

looked across Wally's yard yesterday and seen a girl with a mass of soft, dark curls, he'd been fairly certain he was looking at a Toussaint. A beautiful, delicate Toussaint.

From as far back as he could recall, he'd been warned to stay away from anyone with Toussaint blood in their veins. The men were thieves, and the women thought they were better than anyone else. As his grandmother always said, "Those women walk around with their noses so high, they'll drown in a rainstorm." Then she'd always purse her lips, and add, "But those cats can't resist a Pennington man."

The log split with one chop. He should have listened to grand-mère's warning. If he had, he wouldn't have gone to sleep frustrated.

He split wood for several more hours before he leaned the axe against a stump and pulled a beer from the cooler. He figured he'd split a cord and popped off the top of a bottle of Budweiser. He tipped it back as a white Chevy turned off the highway and headed up the drive. Likely one of his grandmother's club members dropping by to share some gossip, but grand-mère was at her "friend" Boots Butaud's for the day. She would not be home until after dinner.

Blue By You

The Chevy rolled to a stop, and Kasper immediately recognized the mass of dark curls on the driver's side. Blue Butler cut the engine to the car and got out. She wore a silky white blouse, and he could see the lacy straps to her slip beneath. A conservative striped skirt hugged her hips and legs to her knees, and her curls bounced as she moved toward him. She held his sweatshirt in one hand and a big straw hat in the other.

"Hello," she said as she stopped in front of him. "I accidentally took off with your shirt last night."

She handed it to him, and he tossed it on the stump. "You didn't have to drive it over." She probably thought that the shirt she was wearing was all proper, buttoned up to her throat like that. It wasn't. One dunk of water, and it would be totally see-through.

"I was in town, and it's not exactly out of the way." She shoved her hat on her head and looked around. "I've never been here."

If she expected a tour, she was doomed to disappointment. She was a tease. A gorgeous tease, with soft skin and a softer mouth. He was not about to sign up for a repeat of the night before.

"How long are you home?"

47

Why so chatty, and why did she care? Beneath the brim of her hat, her blue eyes looked up into his, and he begrudgingly answered, "I leave day after tomorrow."

"Well, maybe I'll see you around sometime."

He dropped his arms to his sides and tapped the bottle against his hip. "I doubt it." Lord, she was beautiful. All pale skin and blue eyes and bouncy hair. Wearing a shirt meant to be modest but wasn't. That skirt might be on the conservative side, but he'd had a real good look at her legs the day before.

"Too bad." She pulled her pink lips into a frown. "I thought we could be friends. Maybe end this silly thing between our families."

"I've never had a female friend."

She smiled and pointed at herself.

His gaze followed her hand pointing at her breasts beneath that thin blouse and lacy slip. Last night, she'd pushed her breasts and crotch into him, and he'd about gone off in his pants like he was fourteen again. "I don't want a female friend."

Her smile fell. "Any female or just me?"

He didn't want to relive that, nor did he want a friend who he was dying to get naked. "Just you."

"Oh."

One corner of her lips pulled down, and he heard himself explain, "I can't be friends with you after last night." He took a drink and purposely elaborated so she'd get back in her Chevy and go before he tossed her on the hood of her car and crawled on top. "I had to masturbate three times to get rid of my hard-on."

Beneath the brim of her hat, her pale cheeks flushed. "I'm really not a tease, you know."

"I don't know."

"It's just that . . ." She lifted one hand with a slim watch on her thin wrist. "I've been warned off you my entire life. 'Stay away from the Pennington men,' over and over, and I just . . ." She dropped her hand to her side. "I got scared. I've never . . ." She looked down at the toes of her white pumps, hiding her face with her hat.

He raised the bottle to his lips. "You've never?"

"Gone all the way before."

He choked on a mouthful of beer.

"If my first time was with a Pennington, I think generations of Toussaints would come back and haunt me."

He swallowed and wiped drops of beer from his chin. "Jesus. You should have told me instead of going on about how you're a woman."

"I am a woman." She peeked up at him from beneath her hat brim. "I just don't think I should be the first Toussaint to get sexually involved with a Pennington."

A virgin. Jesus, Joseph, and Mary. "You think you're the first?"

"Yes." She raised her face and blinked. "I'm not?"

He shook his head, and said, "Follow me."

"Where?"

"You'll see." He set the bottle on the stump, then took her hand. "Watch your step. There are all kind of bricks from covered wells and old cooking pots. This used to be a working sugar plantation, and some of the old equipment is hidden under weeds and vine."

Blue smiled as she looked at the old plaster covering the house and big columns. His big hand engulfed hers as he pulled her along and pointed out overgrown fields with his free hand. "Some of the old slave quarters are over there. Just dangerous piles of wood nowadays, but I crawled all over them as a kid."

There was pride in his voice. A pride that she understood. No matter how old, no matter how bad the wiring and horrible plumbing, Esterbrook was his home. It was a part of his heart and his soul, just as Dahlia Hall was part of hers.

They walked for about fifteen minutes while he pointed to this and that. Then they stopped in front of a live oak. Old and gnarled and enormous, it had to be at least three hundred years old.

He reached for her hat and tossed it on the ground. "Take off your shoes."

"Why?"

He pointed up.

"I'm wearing a skirt," she pointed out.

"I'll help you. It's not hard. When I was a kid, I nailed some steps on the other side and built a fort up there with the wood I pilfered from Dahlia Hall."

Blue slipped out of her shoes. "Why steal? There's old wood all over Esterbrook."

"Stolen wood is always better." He raised a hand toward the steps nailed into the tree. "You first."

"Are you going to look up my skirt?"

He chuckled. "I'm going to try like hell."

He helped her to the first branch, and they climbed higher. Up more steps, higher to the next cluster of branches. Blue stood on the last step and peered over the top of a large platform secured in the thick limbs. "Will this hold me?"

"Of course." He put his hand on the seat of her behind and shoved one time, pushing her onto the platform.

She looked down at him. "Thank you."

He grinned. "Anytime." He hoisted himself up and helped her to her feet.

"Is this going to hold both of us?" If felt solid, but it had been constructed by a kid.

"Of course. I know how to build things to last." Leaves overhead cast lacy patterns and shaded parts of his face as he pointed to a thick branch. "Look."

She took a few steps and leaned her face closer. In the old bark, someone had carved a heart and placed the initials A. B. T. with T. P. P. inside.

"Did you have a great-great-great-aunt by the name of Abigail Beatrice Toussaint?" He put his arm around her waist, and she had to admit it felt good. Safe and secure and like an anchor.

"Yes, but Abigail joined Sisters of Charity and changed her name to Sister Mary Benedicta." Blue lifted her fingers and traced the letters. "Whose T. P. P.?"

"Thomas Paul Pennington."

"They were in love. Lovers do you think?" She looked up into his face. His beautiful face.

"Probably. This tree would have been about half the size it is now."

"Does everyone in your family know about this?"

"I don't believe so. Thomas died in the war, and I don't think anyone saw it until I was about ten and climbed up in this tree to build my fort."

"I wonder if my aunt joined Sisters of Charity after your uncle died."

He shrugged. "I never investigated it. We lost a lot of family in the war, and we're not absolutely sure when Thomas died."

"That's sad." Blue traced the heart with her fingers. "And tragic."

He looked at her out the corners of his eyes. "Are you getting all girly?"

She nodded. "And romantic."

He slid his arm farther across her waist and brought the front of her skirt to rest against his zipper. "Me too."

"You're feeling girly?"

"Romantic." Against her pelvis, she could feel just how romantic he felt. "You didn't come here today to return my shirt, Blue."

She was pretty sure that's why she'd come. And maybe to catch one last glimpse of him if she could. "Why did I come?"

He lowered his face and softly kissed her lips.

Her breath caught a little in her throat and she lifted her breasts. If she stayed, they'd have sex. She'd known it when she'd seen him by the pile of wood as she'd driven up. All hot and sweaty. If she stayed, she'd succumb to a morally corrupt Pennington, but she wouldn't be the first. She ran her hands up his hard chest, covered in a gray T-shirt. Beneath her touch, his muscles bunched, and his breathing got deep.

"You know what happens if you stay, cher?"

She nodded and rose onto the balls of her feet. "Yes. I know."

His nostrils flared. "Are you sure you want to give me your virginity?"

She smiled. "Are you sure you want to take it?"

He groaned, just above a whisper, "Hell yes." His mouth opened over hers, and his tongue swept inside. He tasted a little like beer and something else. Something she'd never had before last night. Hot, intoxicating, desire focused directly at her. She should be afraid, and she was a little. But mostly she liked the rich, luscious desire pouring from him and all through her. It warmed the pit of her stomach and made her breasts ache.

He fed her wet kisses and reached for the top button on her shirt. His fingers brushed her bare throat and chest, and she pulled away from his mouth so she could breathe.

He opened her silk blouse and pushed it from her shoulders. "Don't be afraid."

Blue looked up into Kasper's dark eyes as her blouse floated to the floor of the fort. "I don't know what to do."

He coaxed one thin strap of her slip aside. "You don't have to know." The other side followed. "I know, Blue. I know how to make it good for you."

She stood in front of him, in the middle of a three-hundred-year-old tree, with her slip down around waist. Her hands on his shoulders curled into fists to keep from hiding herself from his gaze.

"Do you know how many times, as a kid, I dreamed of getting a girl up here." His thumbs brushed her breasts, and her pink nipples tightened so much she ached. "And here you are. Better than anything I could have dreamed." He kissed her and touched her, and everything around her went all hot and steamy. The air. His hands.

His mouth sliding to her breasts. He sucked one nipple, then the other, until her legs felt weak, and she and Kasper sank to their knees.

His breath hit her face as he raised his head and pulled off his shirt. His eyes looked sleepy and shone with lust. His hard chest was covered in dark hair that tickled her sensitive nipples as he wrapped her arms around his back and kissed him. A long, tortured moan rumbled his chest and throat, and she slid her hand to his flat abdomen. She kissed and rubbed against him, tugging at the metal buttons on the fly of his pants. She was mindless, consumed with mindless greed and fiery lust and virgin innocence. Her hands shook and fumbled with the buttons until he put his warm palms over hers and finished the job. He pulled his penis from his pants and underwear and put it in her palm. Hard as steel and hotter than any flesh she'd ever felt before. He moved her hand up and down his soft shaft, and she stared down at their joined hands, fascinated by the size and width and plump head. She'd seen a penis in pictures, but she'd never held one in her hand. She knew that people had been having sex since Adam and Eve, but this looked too big. "I don't think this is going to fit."

He chuckled and unzipped the back of her skirt. "It fits. I promise." He stripped her of the rest of her clothes. "Lie down, Blue. Lie down, and I'll make it so good, you'll only feel pleasure."

She did as he told her, and he did as he promised. He touched between her legs, then spread his wet fingers across her nipples. She moaned and arched her back as he licked her breasts clean.

"You taste good," he whispered, and spread her legs. He moved between her knees and stroked his penis as his dark, hungry eyes looked down into hers. "You're going to like this," he said. He leaned forward, and the plush head of his erection touched her between her legs. It did feel good, and she moaned and bit her lip. Her eyes slid shut as he shoved inside. A stitch of pain pulled her brows together, and she sucked in a breath. His fingers brushed her slick clitoris as he pushed farther inside, giving her pleasure and pain.

His hot breath brushed her check as he leaned over her and ran his fingers through her hair as he buried his penis inside.

"Blue," he whispered against her mouth. "You're so tight. So good." His fingers plowed through her hair. "Are you okay?"

She wasn't sure. She didn't know what she felt most. The pleasure or the pain. But then he moved, carefully, sliding out, then back in, and a fiery friction burned away the pain. "Do that again," she said, her voice a husky whisper. And he did. Again and again. Slow at first. In and out. Telling her how good she felt. How beautiful. The hot push and slick pull and the fiery friction grew.

"Kasper!" she called out.

"Yes. Come for me, cher," he breathed into ear. "Beautiful girl."

She couldn't recall anything feeling this good. She couldn't breathe. She didn't need to breathe. She just wanted more. She moved with him, meeting his thrusts until the fiery friction spread from her thighs and flashed across her skin, and her whole world blew apart.

When it was over, when it was Kasper's turn to cry out and call her name, when his breathing tickled her ear, and his hips stopped, she felt different. When her brain cleared, and all the pieces of her world came back, she felt changed. The pieces the same yet altered somehow.

"You okay?"

She nodded. She was the same person, only

different. She'd made an adult decision. She hadn't considered anyone else's wishes but her own. Anyone else's wants and needs, and the world hadn't ended.

He lifted his face and looked into her eyes. "Say something."

She was no longer a virgin and felt no regret. "How many more times can we do that?"

He smiled, slid out of her body, then back inside. "As many as you like."

The answer was three. They had sex three more times in the old live oak. Three more times until the sun slipped low enough to cast the first shadows of night. Three more times until Kasper stood and helped her dress.

"Maybe we should carve our initials into the tree like Abigail and Thomas," she said, and zipped up the back of her skirt. Kasper glanced up into her face, then returned his attention to the front of her blouse. He concentrated on the buttons and didn't say anything. For the first time since she'd climbed the tree, she felt like she'd been too bold. Stepped over an invisible line. Weird, considering she'd been naked most of the day. "Only without the heart, of course. More like tagging," she assured him.

"I don't have a knife." He finished the last button near the base of her throat.

"Oh."

"I'll meet you here tomorrow around noon." He smiled and pushed her hair from her face. "You bring your gorgeous self and maybe a blanket. I'll bring a knife."

At exactly noon the following day, Blue crawled up into the oak tree. She dragged a blanket with her and sat beneath the old carved heart. She waited in the muggy air, and as the sun got hotter and slid west. She waited in the heat and humidity. She waited until she knew he wasn't coming.

Chapter Four

2013

"Excuse me." The director of tours for Dahlia Hall, Patricia, stood in the doorway of the small office Blue shared with Carolee in the converted carriage house. "Tina McCoy just clocked out."

Blue looked up from the spreadsheet she and Carolee were going over at Carolee's desk. "That makes three times in the past month she's left early." She glanced at her watch. "Her last tour begins in five minutes."

Carolee frowned. "Cramps again?"

Patricia shook her head. "A 'weird eye' this time."

If Tina didn't make such a good Scarlett O'Hara, she would have been fired the second time she left early. "Time for you to get in the dress." She pointed at her friend. "I did it last time."

"Wish I could help you out." Carolee pointed to the stack of work on her desk. "I have to finish the month's account receivables." She frowned. "Sorry."

No she wasn't.

Blue sighed and headed out the door. "Fire Tina," she said, and moved toward the big house. Tourists wandered the gardens, and she said hello before she moved through a back door and walked past the employees' break room to the dressing room. A replica of Scarlett O'Hara's white-and-green barbecue dress hung in a wardrobe closet. Granted, Scarlett was from Georgia, and this was Louisiana. But one thing she'd learned was that to most tourists, a Southern belle was a Southern belle, no matter what state she hailed from.

She quickly undressed and stepped into a hoop skirt. The replica dress was lighter, had less fabric than the original, and not as many layers beneath. The costume was much more functional and zipped up the back. A dark green sash circled the waist, while a matching ribbon tied beneath her chin to keep the flat straw hat on her head.

Blue looked in the full-length mirror one last time, adjusted her breasts in the tight bodice, and headed toward the front of the house. Right on time, she opened the big double doors, and said, "Welcome to Dahlia Hall," with a big smile on her face.

A cluster of about fifteen tourists stood on the white gallery. Gathered was a church group in matching T-shirts, several women Blue assumed were traveling together, a few couples in shorts and flip-flops, and one man who stood apart. Tall, dark, his hair touched the tops of his ears and back of his thick neck. Fine lines creased the corners of his dark eyes.

Kasper Pennington. What did he want?

Blue pushed up the corners of her mouth even higher. "I'm Miss Blue, and we'll be spending the next hour together. If you have a question, just ask."

"Is Blue your real name?" someone wanted to know.

"Yes. I'm named after one of my aunts." She

glanced at Kasper, then stepped out onto the gallery. A slight smile curved his mouth. Last night, she hadn't known how she felt about seeing him again. Today, she was more confused than anything. Why was he at Dahlia Hall? In the last group of the day? What could he possibly want?

Blue began the tour with a history of the land and family and original house. "When Garrard Toussaint brought his bride home, she was not impressed with the original Creole architecture and began renovations that lasted ten years and resulted in the current Creole, Greek Revival style." As she spoke, she was very aware of Kasper's rapt attention. On the columns and fanlight windows, but not really on her. "In 1820, the original mistress, Dahlia Toussaint, added the belvedere on the roof, so she could always have a clear view of the river." Several times, Blue stumbled over her well-rehearsed script, and he smiled even as he ran the tip of his fingers across the shutters.

The tour moved into the house, and Blue waited in the doorway for the last straggler to enter. Of course, it was Kasper.

"What are you doing here?" she asked just above a whisper.

"Apparently, I'm touring your home." He pointed to the group in the entry. "Imagine that."

Yeah. Imagine that. She turned, and continued, "Like most Creole floor plans of the era, there are no hallways at Dahlia Hall. Just suite after suite. The parlors were designed with large pocket doors that could be opened to connect them all to the big foyer for special occasions, like balls or funerals," she said, and took a glance at Kasper, who stood in the gentlemen's parlor, studying the intricate details of the restored murals on the walls.

They moved into the dining room, where family portraits hung on the walls. "This porcelain was brought to the house from Paris as part of Laura Blanchard's dowry in 1850," Blue said as she pointed to a Sheraton sideboard. She lifted her hand to a portrait hanging above the porcelain. "This is Laura."

A deep voice spoke from the back of the room. "Was she a first cousin?"

Blue didn't even have to look at Kasper to know who asked the question. "She was not." She bit her lip to keep from smiling, recalling that time many years ago when she and Kasper had stood at a backyard barbecue arguing over whose family was more inbred. If she recalled, the answer was hers.

For the next hour, she turned up her Southern belle charm and showed the group the big house, grounds, and slave quarters of Dahlia Hall. Usually, she enjoyed showing tourists her home. She was proud of her heritage, but this was by no means a typical group. A former lover stood in the small crowd. Her first lover. The man to whom she'd given her virginity in the cradle of a live oak tree. The man who'd told her to meet him the next day but never showed. She wasn't bitter about that. Not now. Like generations of Southern women before her, she lived though what was thrown at her and moved on. Whether by design or accident or act of God, she lived her life as it came at her.

No, she wasn't bitter, just embarrassed. Even after all these years.

The tour ended under a live oak draped with Spanish moss at the front of the house. The image was totally staged. A Southern belle waving good-bye, the last thing the tourists saw as they jumped back in their buses and cars and minivans.

One vehicle remained in the small parking lot. A Pennington Construction truck, and she could feel Kasper behind her, like a hot electrical current raising the hair on her arms. When the last minivan entered the highway, she turned to see him resting an arm against a low-hanging branch. The shifting shadows from the swaying moss cast patterns across his face and green polo shirt. PENNINGTON CONSTRUCTION was embroidered above the left breast pocket of his shirt, tucked into a pair of Levi's.

"Can I help you with something?"

He stared into her eyes. "You look like Scarlett O'Hara." His gaze slid down her throat to the top of her dress. He grinned before retuning his attention upward to her hair and hat.

Suddenly, she very aware of her breasts pushed from the tight bodice. "Did you come here to stare at my dress?"

"No, I dropped by to say thank you for last night. The dress is lagniappe."

Lagniappe, a little something extra a person didn't expect. Something appreciated. "You could have said thank you without sticking around for the whole tour." She moved toward him and stopped near the low-hanging branch. "You probably have better things to do than listen to my family history."

"I know your family history, and that part about a neighbor's conspiring to steal Dahlia Hall land is complete and utter bullshit."

Blue rested her elbow next his forearm. "Depends on if you believe facts or no 'count fiction."

"Everyone knows the Toussaints come from a long line of pirates and thieves."

"And the Penningtons can't be relied upon to remember the truth due to the pickling effects of Old Crow."

Kasper chuckled and raised his hands to the big green bow beneath her chin. "We only drank Old Crow during Prohibition, when the good stuff was difficult to acquire."

Blue attempted to swat his hands away. "What are you doing?"

"Taking off this stupid hat." He pulled the bow free, then grabbed it from her head. "Last night, you stood in the dark, and I didn't get a good look at you." He handed back the hat. "Today, that kept getting in my way."

She grasped the wide brim against the sudden turmoil in her stomach, and, for several unnerving moments, he stared at her as if he was looking for something. Then he smiled, "There you are."

Beneath her hand, the turmoil in her stomach spread across her skin. "Where else would I be?"

He slid his fingers along her jaw. "You look as I remember."

"Hardly." His fingers sent little shivers across her throat, and she took a step back. She was not eighteen this time. "I am forty."

"I know how old you are." He rested his arm on the branch once more. "You're more beautiful at forty than you were at eighteen."

She tilted her head to the side and frowned. "My momma didn't raise a stupid child."

"It's true." He laughed. "You look more like a woman than a girl."

There had been a day a long time ago that they'd both agreed she was a woman.

"It's a compliment, cher. You look good. Better."

He still looked as good as fresh-baked sin. Tall and filled out with hard muscles, and his hair looked better now. Now that he no longer had the military buzz cut, a dark lock touched his forehead. His dark eyes could still melt a woman, but there was a weariness at the corners. Like he'd seen and done too much in one lifetime.

"Thank you." She straightened, then asked,

before his sugar mouth had a chance at lowering her guard, "So why are you really here, Kasper."

"I told you. To thank you for last night. Grandmère can be a handful, and you put up with her."

"You're welcome." She pushed her hair behind her ears. "You didn't have to join the tour to tell me that."

"I hadn't meant to. I walked up as the tour started, and I stuck around." He shrugged and folded his arms across his wide chest. "It was interesting."

"You were interested in my family history?"

"Your version, yes." He chuckled and held up a hand to stop her outrage. "We'll agree to disagree on that. I'd never been in Dahlia Hall. You've done a really good job restoring the estate. I always wanted to renovate the slave quarters at Esterbrook, but they've deteriorated past their bones."

"I heard you were renovating Esterbrook," she said as if she'd just learned of it. "How's it going?"

"Slow. The sixties were hard on the big house. All that shag carpet." A scowl pulled his dark brows together. "And all those goddamn layers of goddamn wallpaper dating back to 1830 that had to be taken down. The Pennington women were demented about fucking wallpaper."

Blue smiled. "I guess you're not picking out wallpaper now?"

"Hell no." He sighed as if the whole subject wore at him. "Esterbrook is my home. I'm not restoring it to live in a museum. I want to keep as much of the history as possible, but I want a flushing toilet."

Blue knew exactly what he was talking about. The plumbing, no matter how modern, could go cattywampus. She'd had public restrooms built next to the parterre garden, and the low water table was an occasional problem even with the new plumbing.

"Are you living there now?"

"I have a house in Jefferson Parish, but I don't feel right leaving grand-mère alone at Esterbrook. The first floor is almost completed, but the second floor needs a lot of work."

She wondered what his house looked like in Jefferson Parish and if he'd ever lived there with one of his wives. She supposed she could ask, but that was personal information. The less she knew about his personal life, the better. "Well, if you ever need advice on restoration." She took a step back, and her shoulders hit the branch of the tree. "Give me a call. I know a trick or two I could show you."

"What are you doing tomorrow night?"

That soon? He wasn't kidding about getting the house finished. "Nothing."

"Good. I'll pick you up at seven." He took a step toward her and gestured toward her dress. "Wear that."

"What?" She looked down at the ruffles and green ribbon and her breasts pushed together. "Do you want a tour guide?"

He reached for her hand, and she looked up into his brown eyes. "No."

At the warmth of his touch, her pulse kicked up. "I'm filling in for an employee today. She's smaller than I am." For some reason, she felt the need to explain.

"Especially up top." His laughter flashed in his eyes, and she felt herself melt a little. "I want you to come have dinner with me and Miss Sudie."

"Oh. I . . . At Esterbrook?" With the Penningtons? She'd promised herself last night there would be no melting.

His thumb brushed the back of her hand. "Say yes. Grand-mère wants to thank you for your kindness. It would mean a lot to her."

If it had just been him, she would have turned him down flat. There was something dangerous about him. Something that felt unfinished. Something she had no desire to finish, no matter how much he made her stomach feel squishy. "I'd love to have dinner with you and Miss Sudie."

"Good." He dropped her hand. "Bring that dress. It's sexy as hell."

"I'll bring it, but you have to wear it."

Kasper wore a white dress shirt, a beige-and-burgundy tie, and a pair of khaki chinos. He was so handsome. Dark and swarthy, like one of the four fallen angels in her family's old Bible.

Blue raised a glass of wine to her lips. She wore a modest black wrap dress and red, four-inch heels. Nothing sinful about her. "Where's Miss Sudie?"

Kasper smiled. "Detained."

The heels of Blues pumps dug into the new Persian rugs, so different from the threadbare carpets at Dahlia Hall, as they moved to the dining room. She'd been at Esterbrook for almost an hour as Kasper had kept her busy, showing her the renovations he'd done to the home itself and the restorations of the hand-painted ceiling medallions. She could see why his renovations were taking him so long. The workmanship was phenomenal. The fireplace mantels had been removed and refinished, while the iron firebacks had been duplicated and replaced for safety. The bricks inside had been removed, cleaned, and replaced. The walls had been stripped of paper and sanded. They talked about headaches with permits and disposal of toxic materials like lead paint.

"When will Sudie be undetained?"

He pulled out a chair at one end of the long, double-pedestal table with ball and claw feet. The table was set for two, with antique porcelain, fine linen, polished silver, and Lismore crystal. "Later."

She stopped and looked at him across the chair. "Was she ever going to join us?"

"Sure. She made the gumbo." He moved to a sideboard set with a silver serving dish heated by a single Sterno flame. He filled two bowls and looked over his shoulder at her. "Sit, please."

She did, and he set a bowl in front of her.

"When I was sucking up dust in Fallujah or freezing my ass off in the Afghani mountains, I dreamed of grand-mère's seafood gumbo," he said, and took the seat next to her at the head of the table. He placed his linen napkin on his lap. "That and Mississippi mud and bare grass under my feet."

"How long were you in Iraq and Afghanistan?"

He picked up his soup spoon and pulled the cloth from a basket of crisp French bread. The light from the converted gas chandelier cast spears of light across his chest and in his dark hair. "Depends on which time I was deployed." He talked about the hours spent behind fixed optics, looking for anything out of place. A car. A shadow at the wrong time of day. Slight motion against an outcrop of rocks.

The gumbo was delicious. The dark Cajun roux had just the right balance of spices and was served over rice and thick with shrimp and crab. "What was your rank when you retired?" she asked, and took a drink of wine to cool her tongue.

"Gunnery sergeant." He broke off a piece of bread and talked about his friends and the men he'd served with. He refilled her glass, and they ate pecan pie for dessert. She asked about his construction companies, and he told her how and why he'd started each one. They talked mostly of him and his different careers. Blue was fine with that. It kept the conversation platonic. Not personal. Personal could get them in trouble.

"Now that we've covered me," he said, and pushed his bowl away, "let's talk about you."

"Me." She put her fork down and finished her wine. "Nothing to talk about."

He loosened his tie and unbuttoned his collar. "Last time we talked, you were on your way to Tulane."

That had been twenty-two years ago. He remembered. "I pledged Kappa Alpha Theta and graduated with a liberal arts degree." She shrugged and reached for the napkin on her lap. "Married a Sigma Phi, of course. We were married for ten years, divorced five, and have a fifteen-year-old son. He's at his dad's for the summer." She placed the napkin on the table. "Compared to you, I've been a slacker."

He moved behind her chair and pulled it out. "I regret not having children."

She stood and faced him. "It's not too late. You're a man. Find a young wife."

A sad smile pulled at his handsome lips. "I tried that." He took her hand in his, and the warmth of his palm heated hers and spread warmth up her wrist. "Twice."

Yeah. She'd heard.

"I regret those, too. I wasn't a very good husband."

She'd heard that, too.

"Come with me."

She balked. "Where?"

"I want to show you something."

If he pulled down his pants, she was going to punch him in the throat like she'd been taught in self-defense class. "What?"

He pulled her along slightly behind him. "Something I think you'll like."

She thought it only fair to warn him, "If you pull me into your bedroom, I'm giving you a throat punch."

He laughed as they moved up the grand staircase. "Relax. I'm smoother than I used to be. I don't have to pull anyone into my room."

Scary, since he'd been pretty dang smooth.

They continued down a dark hall, and she got an impression of walls stripped to the laths and closed doors. "Watch your step," he said, as they moved past buckets and toward a set of large

French doors. Moonlight shone through the old wavy panes of glass and cast a watery stretch of light on the cypress floor.

"I think you of all people can appreciate the work I've done out here." Kasper dropped her hand to open the doors, and they stepped out onto the heat and humidity of the Louisiana night. The heels of her pumps tapped across the second-floor gallery, totally restored to its original stark white. She put her hand on the rail, and her breath caught in her throat at the parterre garden below. Bigger than the gardens at Dahlia Hall, the hedge design was less detailed, but the fountains were truly grand. Restoring the gardens had been a monumental task and clearly cost a lot of money. He was right, she could appreciate his hard work.

"I'm not finished," he said as he stood next to her. "I want to incorporate the three remaining columns of the pigeonniers."

Of course, Esterbrook's pigeonniers had been built with columns. She turned to look at him through the darkness, and he seemed to be waiting. For a reaction or opinion, as if it mattered to him. "You've done a wonderful job, Kasper." She returned her gaze to the garden below. "Perhaps a smaller formal garden within the columns. Maybe create a Grecian folly with a temple d'amour."

"Or Isis."

"Or you could put in a shrine of St. Jude or Mary." She looked at him. "Even though you're Baptist."

"Which is why I was way more interested in phallic saints than martyrs."

She laughed. "You want to put a phallic saint in your garden?"

His laughter joined hers in the heat and humidity that hung between them. He turned toward her, and he placed his hand on the rail next to hers. "Only if he's packing."

Her laugher turned into a surprised, "What?"

He mistook her outburst for a question. "He can't have an embarrassing package. Anything that can be covered by a leaf. His package has to have some girth."

Her laughter died, and she blinked. Girth? "Like Priapus?"

"Did he have girth?"

"Yes. His 'girth' was heavier than a bag of gold." She was glad of the darkness, so he couldn't see her cheek turn red. If she remembered right, Kasper had girth. Of course, she'd been a virgin,

79

so anything would have felt big. "As if size is important," she hastily added.

"Size is important," he argued, and took her hand from the rail. "Only guys with small dicks say it's not."

That was true. "I don't really want to talk about girth of . . . of . . ."

"Dicks," he helpfully provided, and pulled her toward him. "You brought it up."

"Me?" She put her hand on his chest to stop him. "I did not!"

"You're the one who suggested I put a big phallic shrine in my garden."

No she hadn't. Had she? The warmth of his chest seeped into her skin, and she couldn't think straight.

"Where did you learn about saints with big penises? At your fancy all-girls school?" His warm hands slid up her arms and across her shoulders. "Or Tulane?"

"Priapus was a Greek god. Not a saint." Once again, Blue was struck that he remembered where she want to school. She'd always thought he'd easily forgotten her, as easily as he'd forgotten to meet her the day after she'd given him her virginity. "Kasper."

"Yes, Blue." He placed his hands on the sides of her head and tilted her face up to him.

"You're not thinking about kissing me?"

"No." He lowered his mouth and said against her lips, "I'm past the thinking stage. I'm at do or die."

"But we—" she managed before he kissed her. A full-mouthed kiss with wet lips and smooth tongue. A kiss that stole the heavy breath from her lungs and made her hand slide up his chest to his shoulder and hang on. A kiss that lasted too long to stop. A do-or-die kiss that curled her toes inside her shoes and made her breasts tingle. A kiss that made her want to do it or die.

She pulled back and closed her eyes. She was no longer a girl. She knew what would happen if she continued. She would end up in bed with Kasper Pennington. Again. If she walked away now, she would end up in her own bed. Alone with no regret. Alone with her self-respect.

She opened her eyes and looked at him. At the lust staring back at her, and she melted beneath his gaze. Just like all those years ago, and she reached for his tie.

No one knew she was at Esterbrook. No one would know what she did or didn't do on the dark gallery. And if the past was a predictor of the future, she wouldn't see Kasper for another twenty-two years. He might melt her resistance, but her heart was safe.

She didn't want to be lonely tonight, and self-respect could be very lonely.

Chapter Five

Kasper let out a sigh of relief as Blue pulled at the knot of his tie. He hadn't brought her up to the second-floor gallery to have sex, but it wasn't exactly as if it hadn't crossed his mind. Standing next to her. Looking down at the ground. Just like twenty-two years ago.

He pulled the tie from his collar, and it fell to the ground. To be honest, he'd thought about it the moment he'd picked her up at her house. Probably before. Probably yesterday, when she'd opened the doors to Dahlia Hall looking like the opening scene of every porn movie with a hot Southern belle.

He watched her fingers work the buttons on

his shirt. He liked her hands on him. Liked the way her fingers looked and felt on his skin. She pulled the shirt from his pants and tossed it. A hot, greedy shiver worked its way from the base of his skull down his spine as she ran her palms all over his chest. Her soft touch tightened his testicles and made him hard as the barrel of a gun. He reached for the bow closing her dress at one side of her waist and pulled. The dress fell open, and he pushed the sleeves from her shoulders.

He purposely pinned her arms to her side to keep her hot hands from finishing things before they started. Beneath the dress, she wore a silky black slip, and her hard nipples slid beneath the material as she struggled to untrap her hands. "You're not wearing a bra." He stated the obvious.

"No. The straps ruin the line of the dress." She arched her back in her struggle, and he buried his face in her cleavage. Cleavage he'd stared at the day before like a kid. He rubbed his cheek against her breasts and the hard tips. She gasped, and her struggles stilled. "Let go of my hands," she said. "I want to touch you, too."

He wasn't ready for more of her touch. Ready for it to be over before it began. She made him feel twenty-one again. As if they stood in an oak tree and were picking up were they'd left off twenty-two years ago. Only he had less control this time. He sucked her hard nipples through the silky fabric, and her hands and arms finally broke free. The dress fell to the floor, and one strap of her slip slid down her arm. One nipple popped out, and she ran her fingers through the sides of his hair as he sucked her bare breast. Her little gasp turned him on, and he clutched the bottom of the little black slip and pulled it over her head.

He straightened and looked at her, standing on his gallery, wearing little black panties and red shoes with high heels. "You're a fantasy."

"I'm a real woman." She pulled at his belt and tossed it aside. "A woman who wants to touch you." She unzipped and shoved her hand inside his pants. Her soft palm wrapped around his dick, and she continued, "I want to feel you in my hand and mouth and body." He locked his knees and let her touch him. Let her pull him out and move her hand up and down his shaft. Slow teasing touches until he could stand it no more. Until he felt the urge to throw her down and crawl between her legs. To shove himself inside and not care about her pleasure. Only his. He took her hands from him and spun her around so her back pressed into his chest. "Slow down."

"No," she whispered as she raised her hands and brought his mouth down to her. "Later."

She gave him a long, wet kiss that let him know how much she wanted him. Let him know that she wanted him every bit as much as he wanted her. And he wanted her. In every barbaric beat of his heart. In the darkest place in his soul that demanded he take her now. At certain times in his life, he'd been as barbaric as the enemy he faced. Times when he'd gone to that dark savage place, but he was not a barbarian. He could take his time and draw out the pleasure. Make it better for her, and that was exactly what he meant to do until she shoved her behind into his crotch, and he lost control. He raised his head and gasped for air.

"Blue," he managed. "Grab the rail."

She pushed her panties down and kicked them aside. Then she looked back at him as she bent forward and grabbed the rail. He palmed her smooth behind as his pants and underwear hit the floor. The head of his penis touched the crack of her butt, and he slid his hand between her legs to cup her crotch. "Spread your feet a little bit for me." She was wet and ready and moaned deep in her throat as he parted her and teased her slick flesh. Within the moonlight and the shadows of the house, he positioned himself and slowly slid into the hot pleasure of her body. She was as incredibly tight as he remembered. He sucked in a breath and buried himself, so deep, his thighs slapped her behind. He leaned over her and pushed her curls to one side. He kissed the side of her throat. "You feel good, Blue. As good as I remember." His body covered hers, and she arched her back, pushing her bottom into him, telling him without words that she wanted more. He gave it to her in slow, smooth thrusts. He pulled out and drove inside again. Then again, and his heart beat in his chest and pounded in his head. Hard, like he wanted to pound into her, but he didn't.

"I'm not eighteen, Kasper. I know how I like it now."

"How do you like it?"

"Faster." She spread her feet a little more and hung her head between her shoulders. "Faster makes it hotter. Like a fire inside me that rushes across my skin and ends in an explosion."

Jesus. He straightened, and the moonlight

shone on her bottom like a peach, and he slammed into her. "Mmmm," she moaned, and he plunged into her again and again, faster, hotter, like fire.

A deep groan tore from his throat as he felt the first tightening of her body. Her orgasm pulsed around him, squeezing his erection and pulling a release from deep in his belly. He thrust into her over and over as the most intense pleasure he'd ever felt in his life rippled through his body and spread that fire she'd talked about across his skin. *Mine,* his inner barbarian shouted in his head. He leaned forward and buried his face in her damp neck and dark curls.

All mine.

"Just the parterre garden," Blue said into the telephone. "We never rent the big house for parties." She'd learned that lesson the hard way, when members of Ports of Hope had entered the roped-off areas and one had ended up passed out in great-great-great-great-grandmother's full tester bed! "Yes. We can provide the catering," she continued. "You provide the liquor."

Carolee poked her head into Blue's office. "There's someone here for you."

Blue looked up and covered the receiver. "Who?"

"Me." Kasper spoke from behind Carolee. His gaze met Blue's, and she felt it everywhere all at once. Her heart pinched just a little, and she worried about what that might mean.

Carolee waved her fingers and backed away from the door, leaving Blue alone with the man she'd meant to keep a secret. For the past five nights, they'd met at her cottage or his house. She'd told no one, and no one had seen them together.

Until now.

Blue picked up a pen to keep her hands busy and wrote unnecessary information. What was he doing here? They weren't supposed to meet until tonight. "Thank you for calling." She hung up the phone and looked up at the man who'd been giving her incredible pleasure for almost a week now. And afterward, they talked about his work and hers. Her son and growing up on River Road. They talked about a lot of things, easy, relaxed conversations, but the one thing they never talked about, not directly was that day twenty-two years ago. Perhaps by tacit agreement, they avoided the subject. "This is a surprise."

He shut the door behind him. He wore khaki pants and one of his Pennington Construction polos. "I have something for you."

He handed her a little porcelain box that fit in her palm. A tiny image of a woman with dark curls and wearing a pink hoop skirt had been hand-painted on the top, with Esterbrook clearly behind her.

"I found that today as we went through some of the old furniture in the attic. I thought she looked like you."

Carefully, Blue opened the box. On the underside of the lid, in tiny script, was written, 1840 Miss Louisa Pennington.

"I want you to have it."

"Seriously? This is a family heirloom."

"I don't have a lot of family left these days." He wrapped his arm around her waist and pulled her into his chest.

"I don't know if I can take it. It's worth too much."

He lowered his face to hers, and said against her lips, "I have an ulterior motive." He kissed her, and she wrapped her arms around his neck, the little Limoges box tight in her grasp. She loved the way he kissed her. Long and slow, as if he had all day. Against the front of her dress, she felt his ulterior motive.

She pulled back and smiled. "You missed me."

"Always." He buried his nose in her hair. "I miss you when you're not with me."

She squeezed the box until it cut into her hand. She didn't want him to say things like that. Things that made her stomach go all squishy and her heart ache in her chest. "I know what you miss." She rubbed against him to make light of the chaotic emotions turning her all hot and liquid inside. Things that were in danger of melting her aching heart.

"Not just that," he said against the side of her head. "But that's part of it. You make sex feel better than anyone has in a long time."

"How long?"

"Twenty-two years." She pulled back and looked up in his dark eyes. "Twenty-two years ago," he continued, "when I met a girl with soft curly hair and blue eyes. A girl who gave me her virginity, and I've never forgotten it."

That might have been a romantic speech if not for the elephant in the room they'd been avoiding.

She stepped back, and his hands fell to his sides. "I waited for you."

"When?"

She put the porcelain box on her desk. "That next day in the oak tree." She studied the tiny hand painting and waited. Waited for him to say he'd been in the hospital with something life-threatening that day, or that he'd fallen in a well and couldn't get out. Something.

He was silent, and she looked up. "I know," he said, just above a whisper. "I saw you that day. You wore jeans shorts and brought a yellow blanket."

"You saw me?" A scowl wrinkled her fore-head. "With the blanket. When?"

"When you got there."

"What?" She didn't understand. "You saw me, but you didn't meet me?"

"No. I left for Camp Lejeune a day early."

The anger she hadn't felt at seeing him again after all this time hit her smack in the face. "You had to leave early and couldn't spare ten minutes to let me know? So I didn't wait for you?"

"I didn't have to leave early. I chose to leave a day early."

She didn't understand. Maybe didn't want to understand. "You just left? You left me sitting in that tree for hours? You knew I was there, and you just left?"

"It seemed like the right thing to do at the time."

"For whom?" She pointed at herself. "Not me. The right thing would have been to meet me, and say, 'Hey Blue, I'm leaving for Jacksonville early and can't meet with you. Bye. Have a nice life.' The right thing was *not* leaving me there, sweating to death in that tree. Waiting for you while you were on your way to North Carolina!"

"You're angry. I don't blame you."

"Thanks for not blaming *me*." He reached for her, but she pulled away. "I think you need to go."

"Blue." His hand fell to his side. "Cher, I'm sorry."

She folded her arms across her breasts. To keep from giving him the throat punch he deserved or to protect herself from the punch in her heart, she wasn't sure which. Maybe both.

Blue made herself a Purple Jesus. It wasn't Sunday, but she needed it. She called Billy, who usually cheered her up with his antics, but even her son couldn't lift her mood. Kasper Pennington had somehow managed to make her fall in love with him.

She took a drink and set it on the bedside table as she pulled a short white nightgown over her head. She'd been in love before. With Billy's daddy. She'd loved him madly, but never like this. She picked up the jar and headed into the parlor. Love with her former husband had not happened this fast. Or hard.

She raised the jar to her mouth as someone pounded on her door. There was only one person who had the passcode to get onto the estate.

"Open up, Blue. I'm not leaving."

She believed him and opened the front door. Her stupid heart swelled in her chest. "What do you want Kasper?" She expected him to try and sweet-talk her into letting him inside.

"Let's go."

"What? I'm not going anywhere."

"Get your shoes."

She looked closely into the eyes of the man she knew and noticed a hard glint she'd never noticed there before. She got the impression she was looking at Gunnery Sergeant Pennington, and he did not tolerate disregard of a direct order.

"I'll get them for you." He moved past her and grabbed a pair of rubber boots she wore when she gardened.

"Not those," she protested, as he ushered her out the door. Headlights blinded her as he put his hand in the small of her back and pushed her along to the passenger side of his truck. She balked at climbing inside, and he sighed.

"Please, Blue. I'm tired, but I will hog-tie you."

"Fine." Which, of course, wasn't fine. With her drink in her hand, she climbed inside. He tossed her boots at her feet and shut the door.

Neither spoke as he drove out of Dahlia Hall's gate or as the truck tore up the River Road. He turned off the highway about a mile from Esterbrook and finally piqued Blue's curiosity enough to ask, "Where are we going?"

"Scared?"

Not at all. "Should I be?"

"Maybe."

She drained her Purple Jesus and shoved her feet into her boots. The truck bumped along in the darkness, and the headlights shone on a dirt road, overgrown weeds, and trees. Cypress and live oak. When he finally pulled the truck to a stop, she was feeling kind of buzzed from downing her drink so fast.

She got out and looked around. She knew they were on a strip of property between Dahlia

Hall and Esterbrook, but she wasn't exactly sure where. She glanced around to get her sense of direction, but the darkness and vodka conspired against her.

"Here." Kasper shoved a small but powerful flashlight at her.

She took it and followed after him because what else was she going to do. He was acting like he had a right to be angry. "If I lag behind, are you going to hog-tie me?"

"It's a possibility. Hog-tying is just part of my skill set when it comes to suppressing rebellion."

She glanced about the terrain and the lightning bugs. She smiled at the flits of light that had virtually disappeared after Katrina. But they were back now. Like a lot of New Orleans. Her smile fell when her gaze landed on the outline of the big man in front of her. "Where are we going?"

"Right here." He shined his flashlight on a tree. A live oak tree. "You first."

Apprehension tightened her chest. "You want me to climb this tree? In the dark?" She hadn't been at this spot in twenty-two years, but she knew this tree.

"I'll catch you if you fall."

"Kasper."

"I spent all day putting new steps on the tree," he said, sounding more tired than before. "Now get your ass up there."

She had a feeling that if she didn't climb, he'd throw her over his shoulder and go all Tarzan on her. With her rubber boots on her feet and the flashlight between her teeth, she climbed. Up she went, until she came to the platform that had once been Kasper's childhood fort. In the middle of the floor sat a battery-powered lantern. Like twenty-two years before, she felt a big hand on her butt, pushing her up. Kasper followed and stood in front of her, staring down into her face. By the light of the lantern, she could see he was frowning. His brows pulled together in one dark line. "Are you drunk?"

"No." She was buzzed.

He stared at her for several long moments, then said, "You didn't ask why?"

"What?"

"Today, in your office, you didn't ask me why I left early all those years ago."

She thought the answer was obvious, but since it seemed important to him, she asked, "Why? Why did you leave Kasper?"

"Because I wanted to stay," he said, his voice a low rumble. "And that scared the hell out of me.

For most of my life, I'd wanted to be a scout sniper. I'd dreamed of it as I'd picked off squirrels as a kid. I worked hard to get into sniper school, and I worked hard to earn my Hog's Tooth. The future I wanted for myself was set. I was on my way up; and then I met you." He folded his arms across a clean white T-shirt and looked off into the darkness. "I'd just moved up in rank and was part of the elite forces that I'd always dreamed about. I joined when I was eighteen and planned to serve my whole twenty. Then I met you, and for the first time, I thought about getting out in four years. I was standing at the door of my future, and that scared the shit out of me." He laughed without humor. "I mean, who finds the love of their life at a crawdad feed at the age of twenty-one? That's just ridiculous."

"Kasper." She dropped her flashlight to the floor. It bounced and fell to the ground.

"Who looks through a bunch of steam boiling out of a pot and falls in love with a girl he's never met?"

Tears stung the backs of her eyes as her heart totally melted. She wrapped her arms around him and buried her face in his chest. "Kasper."

"I love you, Blue." He buried his face in the top

of her hair. "I'm sorry I was a coward all those years ago. If you give me the chance, I'll show you that I'm not the man at forty-three that I was at twenty-one. Hell, I am not even the man I was a week ago." He pulled back and cupped her face. "I look at you, and I see something I haven't seen in a very long time. I see a woman I love. I look at you, and I see a future. When I look at you, I see something I've never seen before. I see forever."

"With a Toussaint?"

"With you."

She smiled. "I love you, Kasper."

"Are you sure that's not your Purple Jesus talking?"

She shook her head and laughed. "No. I love you, and I'm sure generations of Penningtons and Toussaints are rolling in their graves."

He pointed his flashlight at a limb in the tree. "Not Abigail and Thomas."

Beneath the old initials, someone had carved a new set. A set much lighter than the first. K. H. P loves B. D. L. B.

"Twenty-two years too late," he said.

"No." She shook her head. "It's perfect." Except he'd transposed two of her initials. But after twenty-two years, the fact that he'd recalled all her names, no matter what order, was impressive.

"When you see our future, what does it look like?" What was she going to tell Billy? Would he be okay? Maybe they should all go to Hawaii. She'd always wanted to go to Hawaii.

"Kids."

"What?" Kids? She'd been thinking of vacation destinations. She looked down, and her hands covered her stomach over her white nightgown. "I'm forty."

"Young enough to have a passel of kids." He laughed at her shock.

"A passel? I already have a teenager!"

"Well, we'll have to talk to him about that. But I think we need some Toussaint-Pennington babies running around."

She was forty. "What if it isn't possible?"

He pushed her hair from her face and looked at her for several heartbeats. "You love me. I didn't think that was possible. Now, anything is possible. I want to spend my life loving you and you loving me. You're it for me, Blue. You're all I need. Anything else is lagniappe."

A nice surprise, like finding love again after twenty-two years. A gift, like finding love with a man who loved like Kasper Pennington.

New York Times bestselling author

RACHEL GIBSON

returns with another deliciously
sexy Marine in her latest novel

RUN TO YOU

Available September 24 from Avon Books!
Read on for an excerpt . . .

Prologue

"Her name is Estella Immaculata Leon-Hollowell and she lives in Miami."

Vince Haven handed his good buddy, Blake Junger, a cold Lone Star, then took a seat behind his battered desk at the Gas and Go. "That's some name."

Blake took a drink and sat across from Vince. "According to Beau, she goes by Stella Leon."

Vince and Blake went back a long way. Blake had graduated BUD/S a year before Vince and they'd been deployed at the same time in Iraq and Afghanistan. While Vince had been forced to retire for medical reasons, Blake had served his full twenty.

Vince opened the folder on his desk and scanned the information that Blake's twin brother, Beau, had compiled for him. Beau had his own personal security business and had his fingers in a lot of different pies. He was one stealth dude and knew how to gather information that your average Joe couldn't access. He could also be trusted to keep all information strictly confidential.

Vince looked at a copy of a birth certificate, and there it was in black and white. His fiancée, Sadie Hollowell, had a sister she hadn't even known about until her father's death, two months ago. A twenty-eight-year-old sister born in Las Cruces, New Mexico. The mother and father listed: Marisol Jacinta Leon and Clive J. Hollowell.

"So, we think she knows Clive is dead." He moved the birth certificate aside to look over a color copy of a Florida driver's license.

"Yeah. She's been told. Told and didn't care."

That was cold but understandable. According to her license, Stella Leon was five feet, one inch and weighted one-fifteen. Which, knowing women as he did, Vince figured meant she was probably closer to one-twenty. She had black hair and blue eyes. He stared at the photo on the license, at the startling blue of her eyes set beneath dark brows. She was an exotic mix of dark and light. Hot and cool. Except for the color of her eyes, she looked nothing like Sadie, who resembled her blond beauty queen mother.

"She works as a . . ." He squinted and put his face closer to the paper to read Beau's handwritten scribbles. ". . . bartender at someplace called Ricky's. Her former careers include lead singer in a band, waitress, cashier, sales, and selling photographs to tourists." He sat back. "Busy girl." Especially since she didn't have to be. She had a big trust fund she drew money out of every month. He read further. Stella Leon had a police record for minor offenses and had lost a small claims lawsuit filed against her by a former landlord.

Vince closed the folder and reached for his beer. He'd give the file to Sadie and let her make the next move. Get in touch with her long-lost sister or just let it go. Sometimes it was best not to tear off a scab. "What's your brother up to these days?" He took a drink, then added, "Besides ferreting out information."

"Usual shit." Blake and Beau were the sons of a former Navy SEAL, William T. Junger. Beau was the older of the two by five minutes, and while

Blake had followed in his father's footsteps, Beau had chosen the Marine Corps. "Running his businesses and trying to stay out of trouble."

"Remember when we met up with Beau in Rome?" Whenever the twins drank too much, they always argued over who had the tougher training program, the Navy SEALs or the RECON Marines. Being a former Navy SEAL himself, Vince had his opinion, but he wouldn't want to have to prove it to Beau Junger.

"Barely. We were piss drunk."

"And got into a fistfight on the train." The brothers' arguments were notorious for being loud, relentless, and sometimes physical. If that happened, it was best just to get out of the way because as Vince had learned, if a guy tried to break up the fight, the Junger boys turned on the peacekeeper. They were two contentious peas from the same pod. Almost identical in every way. Two blond-haired all-American warriors. Iron-souled patriots who'd seen and done a lot and didn't know the word "quit." Vince took another drink. The kind of men a guy wanted at his side in a battle.

Blake laughed and leaned forward. "But get this, he says he's saving himself for marriage."

Vince choked on his beer. "What?" He wiped drops of beer from his chin. "You mean no sex?"

Blake shrugged one of his big shoulders. "Yeah."

"He's not a virgin." There were those who said that Vince had had a thing for easy women. Before he met Sadie, those people would have been right, but no one enjoyed down-with-it girls more than the Junger boys. There was even a wild rumor that the boys had hooked up with a pair of twins they'd met in Taiwan.

"Yeah, I pointed out to him that that particular horse had already left the barn, but he says he's going to remain celibate until he gets married."

"Does he have a woman in mind?"

"No."

"Had some sort of religious conversion?"

"No. He just said the last time he woke up with a woman he didn't know was the last time."

Vince understood that now. Since he'd fallen in love and all that good shit, he understood the difference between sex and sex with a woman he loved. Knew that with the one, the other was better. Knew that it became more than just an act. A need. More than just a physical release, but celibate? "He won't last," Vince predicted.

Blake raised the bottle to his lips. "He seems serious, and the good Lord knows once Beau gets something in his head, he's immovable."

Both the Junger boys were immovable. Loyal and stubborn to the core. Which made them good soldiers.

"He says it's been eight months."

"Eight *months*? And he hasn't gone bat-shit sideways?"

Blake set the empty bottle on the desk. "Some people think he was born bat-shit sideways." He chuckled and flashed the megawatt Junger grin that reached the corners of his eyes. "Me too." He pointed to the folder. "What are you going to do with that information?"

Vince didn't know. He'd have to talk it over with Sadie. Ultimately, it was her call on whether she wanted to contact her long-lost half sister. "Is this Beau's cell number?" He flipped open the file and pointed to the numbers scratched at the bottom of one of the pages.

"Yeah. He has several. Several cell numbers. Several business addresses and a secret lair near Vegas." Blake leaned back in his chair and crossed his arms over his chest. His brows lowered as if an unpleasant memory slid behind his gray eyes. There were guys who thought the Junger brother had spooky eyes. Vince would say they were more hard, like steel, rather than spooky. The good Lord knew they all had hard memories, but just as quickly Blake's expression changed. He flashed his notorious grin, but this time it didn't quite reach his eyes. "So, when are you marrying that hot blonde of yours?"

Chapter One

Back Door Betty Night at Ricky's Rock 'N' Roll Saloon was always the second Thursday of the month. Back Door Betty Night was all about freedom of expression. A pageant of diversity that lured drag queens in from Key West to Biloxi. Lady Gay Gay and Him Kardashian competed for the Back Door crown with the likes of Devine Boxx and Anita Mann. The Back Door crown was one of the more prestigious crowns on the pageant circuit and the competition was always *fierce*.

Back Door Betty Night also meant the bartenders and cocktail waitresses had to dress accordingly and show more skin than usual. In Miami, where short and tight ruled the night, that meant practically naked.

"Lemon!" Stella Leon hollered over Kelly Clarkson's "Stronger" yowling from the bar's speakers. On stage, Kreme Delight did her best impersonation of a shimmering, leather-clad dominatrix. That was the thing about drag queens. They loved sparkles and glitter and girl-power songs. They were more girl than most girls, and loved girl drinks like appletinis and White Russians, but at the same time, they were men. Men didn't tend to order blender drinks. Stella, like most bartenders, hated making blender drinks. They took time and time was money.

"Lemon," a male bartender dressed in tiny white shorts and shimmer hollered back.

The Amy Winehouse bouffant pinned on the top of Stella's head stayed securely anchored as she raised a hand and caught the yellow fruit hurled at her. Around the base of the bouffant fastened to her head, she'd tied a red scarf to cover the many bobby pins holding it in place. On a normal night, her long hair was pulled up off her neck, but tonight she'd left it down and was hot as hell.

She sliced and squeezed and shook cocktail

shakers two at a time. Her breasts jiggled inside her leopard-print bustier, but she wasn't worried about a wardrobe malfunction. The bustier was tight and she wasn't a very busty girl. If anything, she feared the bottom curves of her butt might show beneath her black leather booty shorts and invite comment. Or worse, a slap. Not that that was a huge fear tonight. Tonight the males in the bar weren't interested in *her* ass cheeks. The only person she had to worry about touching her butt was the owner himself. Everyone said Ricky was just "friendly." Yeah, a friendly pervert with fast hands. They also said he had mafia connections. She didn't know if that was true, but he did have "associates" with names like Lefty Lou, Fat Fabian, and Cockeyed Phil. She definitely remained on high alert when Ricky was around. Lucky for her, he didn't usually show up until a few hours before closing, and Stella was usually long gone by three A.M. She wasn't the kind of person to hang out after her shift ended. She wasn't a big drinker, and if she had to be around drunks, she wanted to get paid.

"Stella!"

Stella glanced up from the martinis she set on a tray and smiled. "Anna!" Anna Conda was six feet of statuesque queen all wrapped up in reptilian pleather. Over the past few years, Stella had gotten to know several of the queens fairly well. As with everything in life, some of them she liked. Others, not so much. She genuinely liked Anna, but Anna was moody as hell. Her moods usually depended on her latest boyfriend. "What can I get you?"

"Snake Nuts, of course." The tips of her shiny green lips lilted upward. If it wasn't for Anna's deep voice and big Adam's apple, she might have been pretty enough to pass for a woman. "Put an umbrella in it, honey." Applause broke out as Kreme exited the stage, and Anna turned toward the crowd. "Have you seen Jimmy?"

Jimmy was Anna's leather daddy, although neither was exclusive. Stella grabbed a bottle of vodka, amaretto, and triple sec. "Not yet." She scooped ice into a shaker and added the alcohol and an ounce of lime juice. "He'll probably wander in." Stella glanced at the clock. It was after midnight. One more hour of competition before this month's Back Door Betty was crowned. While the stage was set for the next contestant, a mixed murmur of male voices filled the void left by the music. Besides the employees, few true females filled the bar. Although Back Door Betty Night tended to get loud, it never rose to the same level as a bar packed with real women.

Anna turned back toward Stella. "Your Amy eyeliner looks good."

Stella shook the cocktail, then poured it into a lowball glass. "Thanks. Ivana Cox did it for me." Stella was fairly competent when it came to makeup, but Amy Winehouse eyeliner was beyond her capabilities.

"Ivana's here? I hate that bitch," Anna said without rancor.

Last month she'd loved Ivana. Of course, that had been after more than a few Snake Nuts. "She did my eyebrows, too. With a thread." Stella grabbed a straw and a little pink umbrella and stuck them into the drink.

"Hallelujah. Thank God someone finally got rid of that unibrow." Anna pointed one green fingernail between Stella's eyes.

"It was painful."

Anna's hand fell to the bar and she said in her deep baritone voice, "Honey, until you tuck your banana in your ass crack, don't talk to me about pain."

Stella grimaced and handed Anna her drink.

She didn't have a banana, but she did have an ass crack and she was positive she'd never purposely tuck anything in it. "Do you have an open tab?" She did wear thong underwear, but the string of a thong was nowhere near the size of a banana.

"Yeah."

Stella added the drink to Anna's already impressive bill. "Are you performing tonight?"

"Later. Are you?"

Stella shook her head then looked at the next drink order. House wine and a bottle of Bud. Easy. Sometimes, on a slow night, she took the stage and belted out a few songs. She used to sing in an all-girl band, Random Muse, but the band broke up when the drummer slept with the bass guitarist's boyfriend and the two girls duked it out on stage at the Kandy Kane Lounge in Orlando. Stranding her in Florida several years ago. She liked Florida and ended up staying.

She grabbed a bottle of white wine and poured it into a glass. Stella had never understood why women fought over a man. Or hit each other at all. High on her list of things never to do, right above tucking anything the size of a banana in her ass crack, was getting punched in the head. Call her a baby, but she didn't like pain.

"Break me off a piece of that."

Without looking up and with little interest, Stella asked, "Of what?"

"Of that guy who just came in. Standing next to the Elvis jumpsuit."

Stella glanced through the dimly lit bar to the white suit behind Plexiglas bolted to the wall across from her. Ricky claimed the suit had once belonged to Elvis, but Stella wouldn't be surprised to discover it was as big a fake as the signed Stevie Ray Vaughn Stratocaster above the bar. "The guy in the baseball cap?"

"Yeah. He reminds me of that G.I. Joe guy."

Stella reached into the refrigerator beneath the bar and grabbed a bottle of Bud Light. "What G.I. Joe guy?"

Anna turned back to Stella, and the light above the bar caught in the green glitter in her lashes. "The one in the movie. What's his name . . . ?" Anna raised a hand and snapped her fingers, careful not to snap off her green snakeskin nails. "Tatum . . . something."

"O'Neal?"

"That's a female." She sighed as if Stella was hopeless. "He was also in my all-time favorite movie, *Magic Mike*."

Stella frowned and grabbed a chilled glass. Of course Anna loved *Magic Mike*.

"I wanna bite him. He's yummy."

Stella glanced at the orders on the screen in front of her. She liked Anna, but the queen was a distraction. Distraction slowed her down. The bar was hopping, and slowing down cost money. "Magic Mike?"

"The guy next to the Elvis suit." A frown tugged at the corners of Anna's shiny green lips. "Military. I can tell just by the way he's leaning against the wall."

Stella removed the bottle cap and set it and the glass next to the wine on a tray. A waitress dressed as a zombie Hello Kitty whisked the tray away. Out of all the men in the bar, Stella wondered how Anna noticed the guy standing across the bar. He was dressed in black and blended into the shadows.

"He's straight. A real hard-ass," Anna answered as if she'd read Stella's mind. "And so on edge he's about to explode."

"You can tell all that from here?" Stella could hardly make out his outline as he leaned one shoulder into the lighter wood of the wall. She wouldn't have noticed him at all if Anna hadn't pointed him out. Just one more unsuspecting tourist who'd wandered in off the street. They didn't usually stay long once they figured out they were surrounded by queens and every other flavor of the rainbow.

Anna raised a hand and made a circle with her big palm. "It's in his aura. Straight. Hard-ass. Hot sexual repression." Her lips pursed around the straw and she took a sip of her drink. "Mmm."

Stella didn't believe in auras or any of the woo-woo psychic stuff. Her mother believed enough for both of them and her grandmother was a staunch woo-woo follower. Abuela was into miracles and Marian apparitions and claimed to have once seen the Virgin Mary on a taco chip. Unfortunately, Tio Jorge ate it before she could put it in a shrine.

"I think I'll go say hey. You'd be surprised how many straight men troll for queens."

Actually, she wouldn't. She'd worked at Ricky's too long to be surprised by much. Although that didn't mean she understood men. Gay or straight or anywhere in between. "Could be he is a tourist and just wandered in."

"Maybe, but if there's one bitch to turn a straight man, it's Anna Conda." Anna lowered her drink. "G.I. Joe needs to be thanked for his service, and I'm suddenly feeling patriotic."

Stella rolled her eyes and took an order from a heavyset man with a thick red beard. She poured the Guinness with a perfect head and was rewarded with a five-dollar tip. "Thank you," she said through a smile, and stuffed the bill into the small leather pouch tied around her hips. She had a tip jar, too, but she liked to empty it regularly. There had been too many times when drunks had helped themselves.

She glanced at Anna heading across the bar, blue and green lights blinking in her size thirteen acrylic heels with each step she took.

Roy Orbison's iconic "Pretty Woman" rocked the bar's speakers as Penny Ho strutted the short stage in thigh-high boots and blue-and-white hooker dress, looking remarkably like Julia Roberts. Apparently, "Pretty Woman" was popular among drag queens and tiara tots.

Over the next hour, Stella poured shots, pulled drafts, and gave the martini shakers a workout. By one-thirty, she'd changed out of her four-inch pumps and into her Doc Martens. Even with the thick cushion of the floor matting, her feet had not been able to hold out for more than six hours.

Her old Doc boots were scuffed, but they were worn in, comfortable, and supported her feet.

After Penny Ho, Edith Moorehead took the stage and shimmied in a meat gown to Lady Gaga's "Born This Way." It just went without saying that the dress was an unfortunate choice for a big girl like Edith. Unfortunate and dangerous for the people who got hit with flying flank steak.

Stella fanned her face with a cardboard coaster as she poured a glass of merlot. She was off in half an hour and wanted to get her side work done before the next bartender took her place. In the entertainment district of Miami, bars were open 24/7. Ricky chose to close his between five and ten A.M. because business slowed during those hours, and due to operating costs, he lost money by staying open. And more than groping an unsuspecting female employee, Ricky loved money.

Stella lifted her long hair from the back of her neck and gazed across the bar. Her attention stopped on a couple in fairy wings going at it a few feet from the white Elvis suit. They'd better take it down a notch or one of the bouncers would bounce them. Ricky didn't tolerate excessive PDA or sex in his bar. Not because the man had even a passing acquaintance with anything resembling a moral compass, but because, gay or straight, it was bad for business.

Wedged between the fairy couple and the Elvis suit, Anna's G.I. Joe sat back farther in the shadows. A slash of light cut across his shoulder, wide neck, and chin. The strobe at the end of the stage flashed on his face, his cheeks, and the brim of his hat. By the set of his jaw, he didn't appear happy. A smile twisted a corner of Stella's lips and she shook her head. If the man didn't like queens and in-betweens, he could always leave. The fact that he still sat there, soaking in all the homosexual testosterone surrounding him, likely meant he had a case of "closet gay." Anger was a classic sign, at least that's what she'd heard from homosexual men who were free to be themselves.

After Edith, Anna hit the stage to Robyn's "Do You Know." Her lip-synching was spot-on. Her stage presence was good, but in the end, Kreme Delight won the night and the Back Door Betty crown. Anna stormed off the stage and out the front door. Stella glanced across the room toward the white Elvis suit. G.I. Joe was gone, too. Coincidence?

At one forty-five, she was caught up on most of her side work. She sliced fruit and restocked olives and cherries. She washed down the bar and unloaded the industrial-size dishwasher. At two, she closed out, transferred tabs, and stayed around long enough to get tipped out. She untied her leather tip purse from around her hips and stuffed it into a backpack along with her heels and hairbrush. Out of habit, she took out her Russian Red lipstick. Without a mirror, she applied a perfect swipe across her mouth. Some women liked mascara. Others rouge. Stella was a lipstick girl. Always red, and even though she'd been raised to believe only fast girls wore red, she never went anywhere without ruby-colored lips.

She fished the keys to her maroon PT Cruiser from the backpack. The car had more than one hundred thousand miles on it and needed new shocks and struts. Riding in it jarred the fillings from your teeth, but the air-conditioning worked and that was all Stella cared about.

She said good-bye to the other employees and headed out the back door. June, warm and slushy, pressed into her skin despite the early morning hour. Stella had been born and raised in Las Cruces and was used to some humidity, but summers in Miami were like living in a steam bath, and she'd never quite gotten used to how it lay on her skin and weighted her lungs. Occasionally, she thought about returning home. Then she'd remember why she left, and how much better she liked her life now.

"Little Stella Bella."

She glanced up as she shut the door behind her. Crap. Ricky. "Mr. De Luca."

"Are you leaving so soon?"

"My shift was over half an hour ago."

Ricardo De Luca was a good seven inches taller than Stella and easily outweighed her by a hundred pounds. He always wore traditional guayabera shirts. Sometimes zipped, sometimes buttoned, but always pastel. Tonight it looked like tangerine. "You don't have to leave so soon." His lifestyle had aged him beyond his fifty-three years. He might have been handsome, but too much booze made him pink and bloated. He had a black ponytail and soul patch because he was under the delusion that it made him look younger. It just made him look sad.

"Good night," she said, and stepped around him.

"Some of my friends are meeting me here." He

grabbed her arm, and his booze-soaked breath smacked her across the face. "Party with us."

She took a step back but he didn't release her. Her Mace was in her backpack, and she couldn't get to it one-handed. "I can't." Anxiety crept up her spine and sped up her heart. *Relax. Breathe*, she told herself before her anxiety turned into panic. She hadn't had a full-blown attack in several years. Not since she'd learned how to talk herself out of one. *This is Ricky. He wouldn't hurt you.* But if he tried, she knew how to hurt *him*. She really didn't want to shove the heel of her hand in his nose or her knee in his junk. She wanted to keep her job. "I'm meeting someone," she lied.

"Who? A man? I bet I have more to offer."

She needed her job. She made good money and was good at it. "Let go of my arm, please."

"Why are you always running away?" The lights from the back of the bar shone across the thin layer of sweat above his top lip. "What's your problem?"

"I don't have a problem, Mr. De Luca." And she pointed out rather reasonably, or so she thought, "I'm your employee. You're my boss. It's just not a good idea for us to party together." Then she topped it off with a little flattery. "I'm positive there are a lot of other women who would just love to party with you." She tried to pull away but his grasp tightened. Her keys fell to the ground, and an old familiar fear turned her muscles tight. *Ricky wouldn't hurt me*, she told herself again as she looked into his drunken gaze. He wouldn't hold her against her will.

"If you're nice to me, I'll be nice to you."

"Please let go." Instead, he gave her a hard jerk. She planted her free hand on his chest to keep from falling into him.

"Not yet."

A deep rasp of a voice spoke from behind Ricky. "That's twice." The voice was so chilly it almost cooled the air, and Stella tried in vain to look over Ricky's left shoulder. "Now let her go."

"Fuck off," Ricky said, and turned toward the voice. His grip slid to her wrist and she took a step back. "This is none of your business. Get out of my fucking lot."

"It's hot and I don't want to work up a sweat. I'll give you three seconds."

"I said fuc—" A solid thud snapped Ricky's head back. His grasp on her relaxed and he slid to the ground. Her mouth fell open and she sucked in a startled breath. Her Amy pouf tilted forward as she stared down at the tangerine lump at her feet. She blinked at him several times. What had just happened? Ricky looked like he was out cold. She pushed at his arm with the toe of her boot. Definitely out cold. "Holy frijole y guacamole," she said on a rush of exhaled breath. "You killed him."

"Not hardly."

Stella glanced up from Ricky's tangerine shirt to the big chest covered in a black T-shirt in front of her. Black pants, baseball cap, he was almost swallowed up in the black night like some hulking ninja. She couldn't see his eyes, but she felt his gaze on her face. As cool as his voice and just as direct. There was something familiar about him. "I don't think that was three seconds."

"I get impatient sometimes." He tilted his head to one side and glanced down at Ricky. "This is your boss?"

She looked down at Ricky. He *was* her boss. *Not now.* She couldn't work for him now, which was moot because she was pretty sure she was fired. "Is he going to be okay?" And that made her mad. She had rent and utilities and a car payment.

"Do you care?"

Ricky snored once, twice, and she glanced

126

back up into the shadows beneath the brim of his hat. Square chin and jaw. Thick neck. Big shoulders. Anna's G.I. Joe. Did she care? Probably not as much as she should. "I don't want him to die."

"He's not going to die."

"How do you know?" She'd heard of people dying from one blow to the head.

"Because if I wanted him dead, he'd be dead. He wouldn't be snoring right now."

"Oh." She didn't know anything about the man standing in front of her, but she believed him. "Is Anna out here with you?" She looked behind him at the empty parking lot.

"Who?"

Stella knelt down and quickly grabbed her keys by Ricky's shoulder. She didn't want to touch him, but she paused just long enough to wave her hand in front of his eyes to make sure he was good and truly out. "Ricky?" She peered closer looking for blood. "Mr. De Luca?"

"Who's Anna?"

"Anna Conda." She didn't see blood. Which was probably a good sign.

"I don't know any Anna Conda."

Ricky snored and blew his gross breath on her. She cringed and stood. "The drag queen in the snake gown. You're not out here with her?"

He folded his arms across his big chest and rocked back on his heels. The shadow from the brim of his hat brushed the bow of his scowling top lip. "Negative. There isn't anyone else out here." He pointed to her and then to the ground. "Except you and Numb Nuts."

Sometimes tourists wandered into the lot or parked in it illegally. What did a girl say to a guy who'd knocked out another guy on her behalf? No one had ever come to her defense like that before. "Thank you," she guessed.

"You're welcome."

Why had he? A stranger? G.I. Joe was big. A lot bigger than Ricky, and it didn't look like an ounce of fat would have the audacity to cling to any part of his body. She'd have to jump up to deliver a stunning nose jab or eye poke, and she suddenly felt small. "This is employee parking. What are you doing out here?" She took a step back and slid her pack off her shoulder. Without taking her eyes from his, she slid her finger to the zipper. She didn't want to Mace the guy. That seemed kind of rude, but she would. Mace him, then run like hell. She was pretty fast for a short girl. "You could get towed."

"I'm not going to hurt you, Stella."

That stopped her fingers and brought her up short. "Do I know you?"

"No. I'm here on behalf of a second party."

"Hold on." She held up a hand. "You've been out here waiting for me?"

"Yeah. It took you a while."

"Are you from a collection agency?" She glanced toward the front of the lot, and her PT Cruiser was still in its slot. She didn't have any other outstanding debts.

"No."

If he were going to serve her with a subpoena, he would have when he'd first walked into the bar. "Who is the 'second party' and what do they want?"

"I'll buy you coffee at the café around the corner and we'll talk about it."

"No thanks." She carefully stepped over her boss but kept her eyes on him just in case he woke and grabbed her leg. "Just tell me and let's get this over with." Although she could probably guess.

"A member of your family."

That's what she thought. She was so relieved not to feel Ricky's pervy hand on her leg, she relaxed a fraction. "Tell them I'm not interested."

"Ten minutes in the café." He dropped his hands to his sides and took several steps back. "That's it. And we should get moving before Numb Nuts comes around. I don't like to put a guy down twice in one night. Could cause brain damage."

What a humanitarian. Although she'd really rather not be around when Ricky woke up, either. Or when one of his sleazy "associates" rolled in. Or have G.I. Joe "put him down" again and cause brain damage. Or in Ricky's cause, *more* brain damage.

"And it will save us both the trouble of me knocking on your door tomorrow," he added.

He was as relentless as he looked, and she didn't doubt him. "Ten minutes." She'd rather hear what he had to say in a busy café than at her front door. "I'll give you ten minutes and then I want you to tell my family to leave me alone." Behind her, Ricky snorted and snored, and she looked back at him one last time as she moved toward the street.

"That's all it will take."

She walked beside him from the dark lot into the bright, crazy nightlife of Miami. Tubes of pink and purple neon lit up clubs and Art Deco hotels. Shiny cars with custom rims and booming systems thumped the pavement. Even at three in the morning, the party was still going strong.

"Maybe we should call an ambulance for Ricky," she said as they passed a drunk tourist puking on a neon-blue palm tree.

"He's not that hurt." He moved closest to the street as he dug into a side pocket of his pants.

"He's unconscious," she pointed out.

"Maybe he's a little hurt." He pulled out a cell and punched a few numbers on his phone. "I'm on a traceable. I need you to call Ricky's Rock 'N' Roll Saloon in Miami and tell them there's someone passed out on their back doorstep." He laughed as he took Stella's elbow and turned the corner. The commanding touch was so brief, it was over before she had time to pull away. So brief, yet it left a hot imprint even after he dropped his hand. "Yeah. I'm sure he's drunk." He laughed again. They moved to the curb and he stuck out his arm like a security gate as he looked up and down the street. "I'm headed there in about an hour. It should go down easy." Then he pointed at the café across the street as if he was in command. In charge. The boss.

No one was in charge of Stella. No one commanded her anymore. She was the boss. Not that it mattered. She'd give this guy ten minutes of her time and then it was sayonara, G.I. Joe.

About the Author

New York Times bestseller RACHEL GIBSON lives in Idaho with her husband, three kids, two cats, and a dog of mysterious origin. She began her fiction career at age sixteen, when she ran her car into the side of a hill, retrieved the bumper, and drove to a parking lot, where she strategically scattered the car's broken glass all about. She told her parents she'd been the victim of a hit-and-run, and they believed her. She's been making up stories ever since, although she gets paid better for them nowadays.

Visit www.AuthorTracker.com for exclusive information on your favorite HarperCollins authors.